AF489520

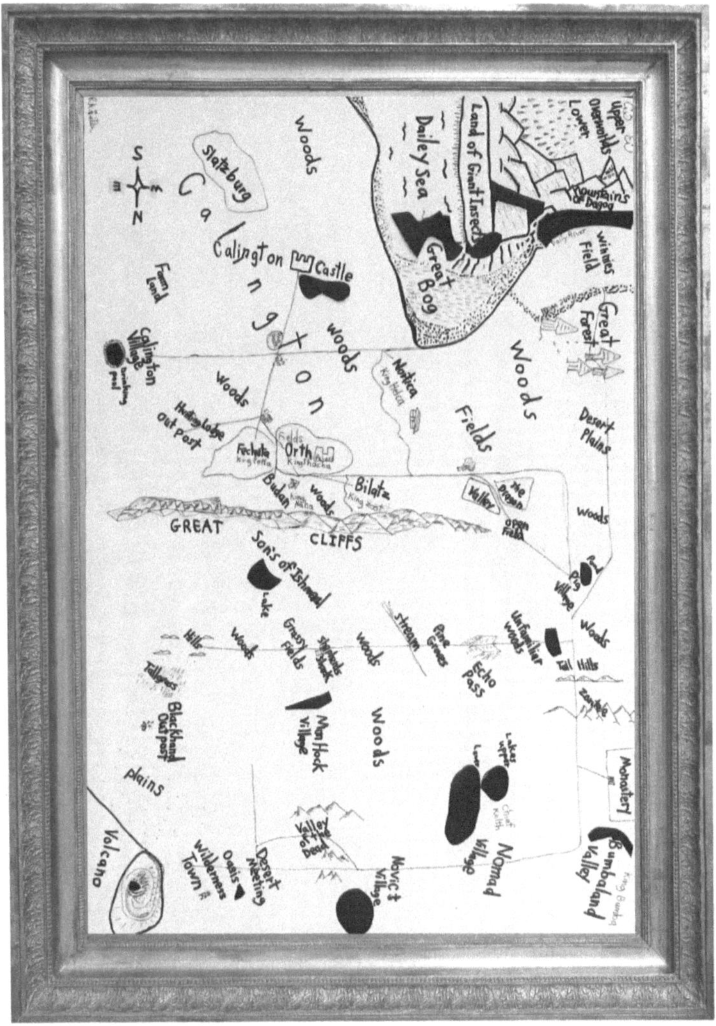

S W E N (compass)
Galington
Slatzburg
Woods
Dailey Sea
Land of Great Insects
Upper Overworlds
Lower
Mountains of Bagog
Winnies Field
Great Bog
Calington Castle
Farm Land
Woods
Calington Village
breeding pool
Hunting lodge out post
Woods
Valley River
Great Forest
Woods
Mortica King Helta
Fields
Desert Plains
Fechita Regions
Orth King Hacka
Fields
Budah King Nitha
Bilatz King Zog
Woods
Valley
The Dream
open field
Woods
GREAT CLIFFS
Son's of Ishmeal

Calington Castle IX

"Friendship"

R. A. Feller

ISBN 979-8-9894920-3-9 (paperback)
ISBN 979-8-9894920-2-2 (eBook)

Printed in the United States of America

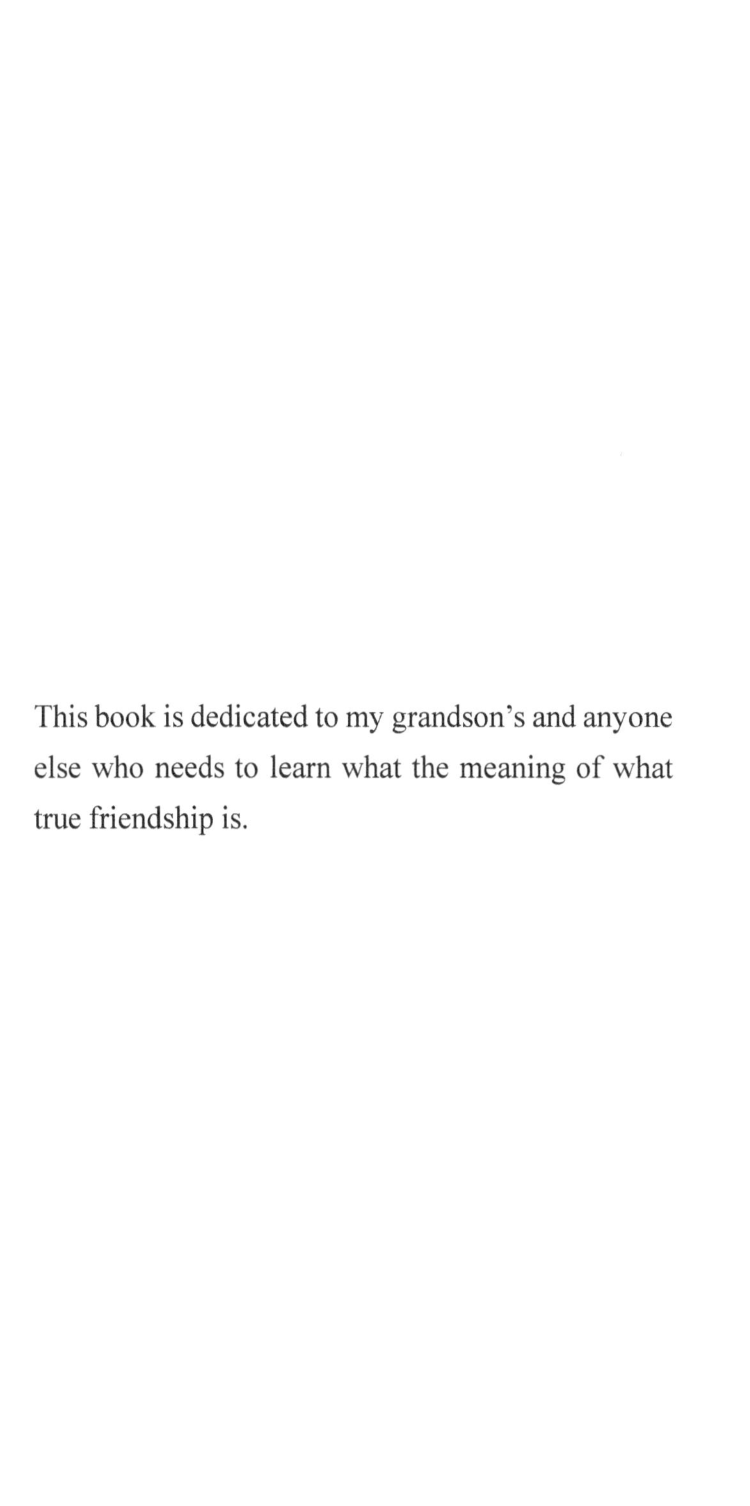

This book is dedicated to my grandson's and anyone else who needs to learn what the meaning of what true friendship is.

What is a Friend?

Eyes behold threads within the pattern of a blanket. A gentle breeze tries to disturb it, but only some short tassels on its edge are moved. Seasoned in his years, King Liam is sitting out on the castle grounds enjoying the warmth of a late afternoon sun when his grandson comes to him in tears, "What's the matter, Ronan?"

"I can't seem to find the right kind of friends."

"Well, if it's any consolation to you, we'll always be friends. Now, what happened that has you so upset?"

I was in the village and there was a boy who came up to me and I thought he was my friend, but without warning he shoved me to the ground …"

"…Ronan, there are those who live to receive life from The Great One's love in a full relationship with Him, those who are on the way to understanding what this means, and those who walk in the dark. I believe the one who pushed you had been led to believe that he could see, but was really frightened into being lost. For when one is inside themselves without any sight, they blindly lash out in fear and miss doing what is right. It is unknown what to do with spirits when confusion is near as they mislead by keeping light darkened in the air."

Liam's grandson dries his tears with the sleeves of his shirt and looking over, says, "I do not understand. Can you tell me more?"

While wiping the remainder of his tears 'til dry on his face, his grandfather explains, "Look here upon my blanket. Do you see the different colors within its design?"

"Yes, but what does this have to do with friends?"

"Let us start out with the fine line of yellow. Remember your first encounter with the glory of

God's love and how much joy it brought you when you were just two?"

"I see. The color yellow must mean having The Great One's Spirit of joy. Yet there is so little yellow and so much red, green, and black and so many of the squares that blend together."

"Ronan, you are fortunate to have come into the yellow at such a young age. Yet there are those who live in the darker places of the black that cannot see they are being used to blend in with the other colors to try and put out the shining of your joy in the yellow."

"Do any of the other colors have meaning beside the yellow and the black, grandfather?"

"The red represents that sometimes we have to suffer to keep our joy in order to remain in the yellow. The shades of green tell of how others grow through different stages, like a green bud before bloom into a yellow flower."

"I understand now, grandfather. The boy who pushed me down tried to interfere with my shining in the yellow. He couldn't see that he was being used by the dark squares to try to put out my joy."

"…And the color red?"

"…My suffering to remain in the yellow must happen due to the joy that God gives from my friendship while growing through the shades of green and other mixed colors with Him."

"I'm glad you understand that love concerns itself with suffering sometimes, for I do not know how much longer you'll be here at the castle with us. I don't know if you've noticed your mother's strange behavior. Being my daughter, as hard as I find it to believe, she was never introduced into an understanding of the yellow and this has influenced her into the darkness of the pattern of the black.

No matter what, we must continue to pray for her to fully know The Great One, that she will no longer dwell in the dimness of lies of shadow shades by believing there is life in the them while in the dark. So, should you ever be taken from this place, do not harden your heart towards her, but pray for her to know the joy of your light instead. Though in telling you this, understand to respect her position as this will give her a desire to listen to what you have to say. Yet guard your heart and pay attention with eyes fixed on the flower of your light of joy as wisdom would not have you do anything against a life of living in the yellow."

"Are you saying that my mother is a witch?"

"All who are in rebellion to the balance of truth and love are unaware that the simple pass on and get punished. It is from a lack of understanding light that all walk under the spell of spirit dragons that stalk the night. Should you find yourself in times of trouble by any shadows, pray to remain in the yellow of the bright."

"I will pray for both me and her, grandfather."

"I know it will be hard to stand up against those who come at you while they live in the dark at times, but always ask for wisdom and The Great One shall teach you life."

"What should I do about the boy who pushed me down if I encounter him again?"

"Ronan, as you find your way through the different patterns of people growing in time, there will be moments of discovering nuggets of truth that will enlighten your mind. Watch carefully how everyone behaves before you speak and your understanding of life will grow. For when you have a seed and care for it, you can tell when a weed comes to choke. The spirit world is much like this. For The Great One, as Creator, protects all thoughts while watching over them that they grow to enhance a life in His garden of love. Weeds try to crowd and draw life from God's thoughts by confusing a plant, but if they stay focused on the truth of the Spirit of love, life will sprout into the eternal by questioning until answers come."

"I remember watching the gardeners pull weeds from around the flowers to prevent them from being crowded out. I always thought that it was to make them look good on the grounds, but now I under-stand the deeper meaning of their purpose of work. It is to protect and preserve the flowers so they won't lose the colors of their life."

"So, how would you handle another who repeat-edly tries to crowd you in the future that has been infested with weeds in the garden of His thoughts?"

"First, I would water him with prayers of love to make sure that I shall not lose my patience. I now understand why verses from the *Book of Life* are so important, for I have spoken what they've taught."

King Liam looks to his grandson with a gaze and a tear in his eye.

"Why are you crying, grandfather?"

"I am not crying but rejoicing."

"I don't understand."

"Your taste for the passion of The Great One's words has been ignited and will now protect you throughout your life.

"How?"

"You have a light that shall guide and protect your High King's heritage and now you shall always live within the light."

"I see with sight. Walk in the light while you have the light, so that darkness will not overtake you."

"Brilliance has captured your mind and heart this day!"

"I understand your happy tears now, grandfather."

"Having this light shall always guide you into doing what is right if you pay careful attention.

For the Great One speaks to us throughout all our actions and spoken words and sometimes by the laws of nature which surround as they contain the ideas of life for everyone around. Now what wisdom would you use after prayer if you found yourself in this position again?"

"For a start, wisdom tells me not to play too far from the grounds without an escort and that I must be more aware of my surroundings."

"You've answered wiser than I when I was pushed …"

"…You were pushed, grandfather?"

"Of course! Everyone is pushed or tested in one way or another, but it must always be remembered that we have a divine purpose to our lives. If this is remembered in these situations, our eyes will forever be kept upon the light we walk in. A choice is ever set before us to walk in darkness or in light. Remember, there are consequences for our actions if we do not guard our tender hearts."

"What did you do when you were tested?"

"I remembered the verse, "Be angry and sin not, do not let the sun go down on your wrath," which saved my life when I had a knife held to my throat during a robbery once. For if I had failed the test by acting in anger, I could have lost my life in addition to my possessions and been killed in darkness rather than remain in light. You would not be here if I had chosen the darkness of flesh over my purpose of vision in life."

"But I feel like I lost my true self."

"Did you?"

"What do you mean?"

"I would say that you set a better example by choosing not to fight."

"Then when do you fight?"

"After prayer, if God's Spirit comes upon you, He will deliver you by His might. Otherwise, continue to live by the words from the *Book of Life* and what they point by drawing from the root of its eternal vine on the tree of life."

"Is there anymore wisdom that you've experienced on the matter of friendships in your life?"

"I have learned that I had to be a friend to myself first before I could be a friend to others."

"I don't understand."

"Oh, I believe that you do."

"How?"

"Have you not just discovered walking in the light?"

"Yes!"

"Well, walking in the light allows you to see and know yourself. For within this light, you can understand that The Great One loved us enough to give us His light to see and know ourselves as the *Book of Life* states, "We love because God first loved us." The Great One as creator and God has loved and embraced us with His warmth that we may see the truth within His light and this allows us to be a friend to ourselves as it is life."

"I see the light in what you say, grandfather. For in knowing myself, I can see how I want to be treated to show myself a friend to others."

"If you do this, even when you find yourself in bad company, which will try to corrupt your good character, you'll stand firm in the face of this adversity and shine your light within the darkness of any crowd."

"I'm learning much wisdom this day as I feel my roots spread out in truth and know that I am growing in the warmth of love."

"You shall further discover that it is easier to learn when you're young. For as people grow older they become set in patterns, which have blown them outside of having peace within themselves. In discovering everyone is in a hurry to go no place fast, you'll see that they shall not break the barrier of the heights and depth of time nor escape back into eternity as you've just described. For in the spreading of your roots and growing in the warmth of slowing down, you'll embrace more light of love inside the breadth that passes within time 'til shattered out of a freefall. Now, we are able to land on the firm foundation of the Christ who lifts us up when standing in His light. So continue slowing down to grow while at rest and the foundation of God's peace will not cease. For when we went no place fast, we could not catch up with God and His power of love to emanate from us as we were not within His kingdom. He has filled us to overflow. As within His presence to touch others, I am left in awe while watching how He uses me to burn away weeds. I have watched others come into bloom by His light and it is precious in my sight."

"Tell me more stories from what has happened from your past, so that I may grow from them to see more of our Great One's truth."

"In the beginning of my relationship with father, King Henry, he was not available to me and with Queen Mary just as busy at court, I really did not have much in the way of guidance in our castle. After becoming the joke of conversation, which I overheard in bits of gossip, lacking in understanding, I only laughed along with them. Back then, I did not realize that many of my friends were jealous of me and were really abusive enemies behind their deceitful smiles. How blind we can be when we run from our pain unaware that it's there? I tried to enter into friendships without understanding what love was many times. I only got pain in its place while believing it was love and even though it added to my darkness, I thought that getting attention was good."

Ronan hugs King Liam, saying, "Oh grandfather, I am so sorry."

"Steady now, for it was a long time ago and during this time, God was preparing me to be a wise king. The Great One was training me to understand all walks of life one lesson at a time.

It wasn't before long your uncle Edward grew to give me a hug and in him I found acceptance. Bit by bit things started to make sense to me in the midst of my commotion and unrest. I was slow in the beginning but my warped point of view, which took me through empty spaces where I watched life pass me by, gradually became filled in as I discovered how to hug myself and knew that somehow God was holding me from within. Then all at once, I knew where love began."

Liam's grandson gives himself a hug and pauses for a moment, "I understand, grandfather!"

Though at this point, Ronan, I still did not see my great value on how I would become effective in touching many lives as there just wasn't enough of me together, but I tasted, God is good. My relationship with The Great One had begun as did my journey to love."

Ronan holds grandfather tightly again.

"I started to see things very differently as do you my grandson. You will find your own space apart from a crowd and start to grow with a vision that will be valuable to our High King and others, too. Although, not very focused now, you'll soon overcome what holds you back. There were limitations in the midst of turmoil that surrounded, but you will grow in your relationship with Him 'til more freedom is found in being who God created you to be. For, He has called you to be His friend by teaching you what love is and this will protect you from going where love is not."

"What do you mean?"

"There will be more perils as you come to know more of yourself before the light of God. Be careful. For when you try to avoid the obvious ones that will do you harm, it can blind you to see what is coming next in the way of friendships. Deceptive friends do not take the time to listen to get to know you but what they can get out of you. They'll lie to get their needs met in terms of what you know or have, and not who you are as a person. So keep your eyes centered on the character of Christ as described in the *Book of Life*. Then you'll stay balanced in your sight and figure out the characters of who you are meeting when they do not reflect His loving life."

"How did you learn this?"

"Coins went missing when we were playing hide and seek. I got blamed as friends suddenly disappeared to my dismay. There was just not any good examples of how to behave. Later on, the healer came into the castle and introduced me to our priests. They taught me how to be grateful before the marriage supper of the lamb, which made me aware of His presence when receiving Him in the Holy Eucharist. Later came the *Book of Life*, which verse helped me to better understand our Bridegroom and Christ. After I was baptized into the church, His Spirit came and made me a part of His bride."

"I have been learning that rightly dividing the word of truth from this *Book* has to do with *its* words pointing to the lamb of God's Eucharistic sacrifice too, grandfather."

"You must learn that all of creation glorifies The Great One as Creator as well. For all creation has a message about how the Creator brings completion to us as His bride by sacrificing Himself while alive. So know that while in fellowship with the Holy Spirit of Light, He completes our spiritual cycle which kept all broken from the bloodline that was originally pure in fullness of life. For the power of our Christ's blood resurrects, giving all who receive with understanding the power of eternal life."

"I see now. Truth always remains consistent and grows to give us better sight by drawing closer to His light. Knowing something we can build upon for all to line up right sets us free when receiving the stability of eternal life. For in knowing what is real lifts all to new heights. As when God is in control, His confidence remains in me to see to leave the dark and know just how to grow within the stages of my growth in every fruit that I shall bear."

"When consistent in this truth that doth not change, you shall always be found correct. For this is what allows us to grow to understand all within the pattern of His timing. Darkness tries to hold us without the seed of resurrection. Yet when we take our thoughts captive by slowing them down within stillness, all taste what was outside of motion as we now burn through everything not of light by confronting its power with the blood of Christ. I gradually came out from the fog of my behavior that seemed so right, but my pattern was wrong while drowning in my surroundings and all I knew to hold me together for many a season became dull not bright. It was a scary thought to let go of the world I knew, but I had reason for why my life had become worthless from being whipped by winds that tore into me. Now outside myself from within, I discovered many discomforts and knew I was worth more, so I took action."

"What did you do?"

"I questioned everything that had control over my life and realized how unsteady I was 'til remembering my first touch by The Great One's love. Keeping my peace, it welled up into a joy that became my strength 'til my knees no longer buckled.

"I felt uneasy as well when I got pushed. It was a horrible feeling!"

" …And it will remain horrible until the Lord strengthens you by the truth of His wisdom from within. You'll always feel the heat from your abusers that lurk in the dark 'til the confidence of God shines brighter inside you than the world in which we live. For the glory light of His kingdom outshines the spirits that live in the dark by truth interpreted correctly, which lives inside verse from the *Book of Life*."

"How am I to look to God and not to what hides in our culture as an abuser?"

"The Great One's Spirit will always overrule anything that lives in the dark even while you're learning."

"I understand what you say, grandfather, yet my heart still fears the darkness that I know I must face."

"Eyes will be upon you to hold you to who you were, but when the time comes The Great One and Christ will prove you true."

"I feel my vision has changed by your words as the Lord now has my confidence and I desire to know Him more."

"Then pray and you shall know Him more before you face each battle. Every stronghold of darkness will only be defeated by His light. So stay true and your conscience shall never trouble you. For while walking in the light if you guard your heart, truth will be one in knowing the faith of your relationship with Him. Deflecting any eyes that lay in darkness 'til Christ's glory shall deliver by shining through."

Ronan just stands and stares as if looking into the dark.

"I see you are yet afraid of what lay in the secret of your heart, it festers. I know this well from what held me in an off-balanced love while practicing what I did not understand. For I walked in the dark at one time, too. Yes, I was not righteous, for God was not within my heart. Yet when I found Him, He became my friend and accepted me for who I am. He spoke gently, telling my heart that it was okay to be me and this encouraged drawing nearer to Him. I was made more stable in close convictions to see through darkness of guilty constrictions. I finally grew to where my identity knew Him in truth. Then through dark flames of trials, His light was sparked as always the proven greater friend."

"Thank you, grandfather."

"Wait! Don't thank me. Trust in your Lord, for He has arranged everything to know Him more. For after you have had many hardships in your life, you will find that they were a pathway to have an even greater peace as you grow to know Him more, too."

"You're saying, The Great One arranged it for me to get pushed."

"We live in a fallen world, Ronan. Because of this you will find yourself in many situations that will trouble your mind. Remember that it is stated in the *Book of Life*, "It rains on the just and the unjust?""

"This is a terrible verse."

"No, it is not. For we now walk in the light of a dark world where we have the privilege of learning that God is our friend."

"My fear of what was hiding in my heart has left me. Having more light within my sight, I have taken the friendship of God's hand."

"Darkness has ways of passing itself off as light. So, be cautious, grandson. For whatever bids for our hearts in place of God's love is a deception in the making. Generations can be altered by a single choice. Make sure that yours are not done in commotion, but in the timing of peace which rewards with God's wisdom."

"Are you referring to Ishmael and Issac by Abrahams choice that has led many to battle because of divisions where wars are being fought unto this day?"

"I see that you are well read and versed in the *Book of Life* for one so young."

"I have discovered that knowing its word is one thing but to fully understand it is another."

"The fullness of wisdom will come in The Great One's timing. Though waiting can be difficult at times, God always blesses best when decisions are made while at rest."

"I am glad I came to you, grandfather."

"Did you come or were you sent by love?"

"I am still learning the mystery of God's ways."

"Everything was established by the truth of living blood from before the fall of man, but Adam put himself to death by believing in a lie. A world of darkness has been opened by this door, which has placed us all in a world with a bloodline that dies while trapped in the realm we now know as time."

"Understanding has come to me. I see that I have been justified by The Christ and know how His restraints of protection are freedom as I am not bound by darkness any longer but love. I have been bought by His own living blood while following the truth of His great love and am kept in the balance of a pleasant place by His own hand. I remain unscratched while in a world of disharmony, for I have learned to stand while no longer holding onto the dark parts of it."

"You shall next tread on the head of serpents and scorpions that hide in many dark places of the abyss. For in not being of this world, you have eternal life. Move slowly and you will discover you have full feelings to enjoy a complete life. Yes, by keeping your center of balance of trust in the Christ, your thoughts and emotions will at last reflect His glory as long as you are free of the spirits that cause strife which had blocked you from the glory of bright light."

"I will not handle any pressures by looking at what can sway me into uneasy choices any longer. For I know that God's hand is able to hold back the adversary. He stands me upright by His light and as the Christ, He has given me an everlasting life. My trust is in Him who is able to deliver from beyond the breadth while in the waves of time as He shall not allow me to be shaken by its waves of corruption any longer. For He is stability itself."

"By sensing when problems arise, you shall not be bound. Truth has gained you growth as your space has been enlarged to where wisdom has become your friend."

"Your words have sharpened me to cut through any fabric that restrains. The warp of any lie cannot withstand Your strength. What can be compared to the well-spring of Your life? There is no denying when evil is present as its pressures are a destructive force. Though when I call upon the might of Your name all of commotion subsides in the pale comparison of the beauty of Your gentleness my Lord. Grandfather, I have been with The Great One in the heights of His glory."

"Now you are protected against the dragon that will try to turn the tide of your heart from light to dark. Though do not be swayed by the words that I say. For if pride should enter in you shall be ripped apart."

"I will be mindful not to cross thoughts of light with dark. For if I enter into strife, there can be a darkness to invite death instead of life."

"You are being guided by God's light."

King Liam watches as the Holy Spirit of The Great One brings full light to Ronan's eyes as his countenance becomes radiant before giving proclamation, "He is a friend that never forces me to do anything against my will. Instead, by revealing His deeper love about Himself, He prevents me from doing wrong. He listens to what I have to say, with forgiveness in His heart, counsels me when troubled, and prays reconciliation on His cross. As a door held open to eternal life, He brings peace to every mind to put an end to any strife. The pattern of His character protects those who love the truth and taking in all the facts they draw conclusions 'til all sits right. Though when a person is not honest, preferring darkness rather than light, God still respects their choice. Yet how can one improve themself without any sight of light, unless known by patient love? For someone cannot be encouraged while they feel they're being shoved.

In our true friendship with God, we always grow to touch His heart. For when no longer restless, there's an arrival in each new moment of perpetual life. He is there in each stage of completion within His timing as our friend, for The Great One never ends."

King Liam is in tears when Ronan stops speaking, "Grandfather, "What was your first true friend like?"

Story of a True Friend

King Liam looks to his grandson and shares what is on his heart, "After encountering those who did not respect me, I discovered what are called boundaries. They helped me to see when someone was trying to pressure me into a bad decision. It took time, but gradually I could tell when someone was disrupting my peace. For when turning my eyes towards the Great One more and more, I could tell the differences between His bond and when someone did not know love.

Because we are God's Children, He is our Father and wants to establish a full relationship with us first as our Lord that we can go to Him in times of trouble. Then while building relations with Him, we are placed most effectively in His kingdom here on earth in each stage of our growth while being prepared as His intimate friend. Seeking to improve my life with Him better helps me to understand love for healthier relationships which has helped others along my journey according to His appointed timing.

I shared this to help you better understand how I met my first real friend."

"I am listening, grandfather."

"A little after your Uncle Edward was born, a tribe from the north of Ostrog called Bumbaland yielded a king named Bacali. He came seeking aid as times were hard for him and His people, but he brought something in return that was worth more than whatever we could have given him in return."

"What was that?"

"My first real friend, as King Bacali's son named Bumba was with him."

"How did you two meet?"

"Funny you should ask, but it really wasn't so funny to him."

"What happened?"

"Not knowing any better I walked up to him and asked, 'How come you're black?'"

"I bleed red the same as you."

"Sorry, I didn't realize."

"It's just the color of my skin that is different."

"My name is, Liam."

"They call me, Bumba."

"Come on, let me show you around the castle."

"I must check with my father, 'Is it okay, Bacali?'"

King Bacali looked at my father who nodded his head and smiled with a single word, "Certainly!"

Bacali had a look in his eye of apprehension 'til my father said, "I'll have sergeant James from the royal guard keep an eye on them." Bacali smiled and all was affirmed. I had my first real friend adventure. I showed Bumba around as sergeant James kept watch, looking on.

"Did you see Bumba again?"

"Yes, many times. I even traveled to Bumbaland as I got older with sergeant James by my side. Traveling throughout the lands became key later on to me sharing my faith with many neighboring tribes."

"Wow! I wish I could have been around during those days."

"Do not trouble yourself, Ronan. For If I know The Great One, I am sure that you are going to have a full life."

"Did your father determine whether or not to help out Bumba's tribe that day?"

"My father, King Henry, was both very wise and compassionate."

"I would have liked to have met him."

"In a way you have by knowing me, for I am of my father like the pattern in my quilt containing many colors. The friends I have met along the way have helped to shape me, too."

"Did making your first friend help you to make friends with others?"

"Ronan, You ask a very good question. Not only did it help me to make other friends but it taught me how to have something called discernment as well. For when you have a loyal bond with a friend, it sparks forth love and a respect of where you can comprehend what is untrue and so starts the beginning of discernment.

"I see, grandfather. First, you must learn to love the truth before you can test it."

"Then you will live it, Ronan."

"I will hold on to what you say as I am learning to know that truth sparks a light which gives flavors of life."

"What is true holds a firm foundation, which allows you to build a life that will hold. Then when you place your words line upon line like bricks in mortar, you shall have a life that will not fail you for lack of wisdom."

"I am still young and you have had a life time of learning to live what is true. Perhaps you could share some more wisdom on what it is to understand living in the truth."

"You have a brighter mind than I. For when I was your age, I would run around collecting shiny stones and give them all to my mother out of love. Later on in my years, I saw how my father examined everything down to the last detail. Then while observing him, I discovered God. The shiny things I collected for my mom and gave away out of love showed me how father did the same thing, but in a different way."

"How so?"

"I realized that he was collecting the brightness of truth which he would carry with him forever. The glory light of God shown upon him towards the end of his life, just like when I was young and we both knew that what was inside him would last throughout all eternity."

"Did you ever ask Him what he found that caused him to glow from within, Grandfather?"

"It was his love for learning how all created things testified of a Living Creator of everything and learning about Him in creation helped me to better understand His Son."

Ronan's eyes light with revelation, "All of creation doth cry out and testify of The Great One. For He was there in the beginning with living blood to bring us all into being. He must have lost sight of the living blood line and light of all men as their are many who die without any understanding of it."

"Well, I see you have been talking with the monsignor while he was here this week as you do sound like many of His words."

"Grandfather?"

"What is it, Ronan?"

"We all sharpen each other. Don't we?"

"It is in learning to be grateful to God in every-thing, that we can tell when someone is not in His pattern. For there are those who do not shine with the light of His love and remain dim from their lack of understanding life."

"So, then we must be aware of His presence to know Him as an ever present help in time of need?"

"Ronan, it takes precious time to really get to know The Great one. For what you see off in the distant future, you cannot go to right now, but must grow to with each step you take. Know as you grow in your relationship with Him, your faith will take you to meet Him on the heights of His mountain."

"So, that's how you climb out of a shadow of death. I shall wait on Him from now on."

"We always climb in stages, but first The Great One has to teach us the craft of using the tools of His established spiritual laws, which trains us to see that we are in need and this gives us reason to climb."

"Would this have anything to do with the boy who pushed me down?"

"Well, have you experienced discouragement, rejection, or confusing circumstances of pain from it?"

"Yes! I see. These were my reasons for coming to you."

"We have an established trust that evil will try and break, Ronan."

"How?

"It always tries to deceive through misunderstandings. Or, perhaps we will be separated from each other, but no matter what our bond of love will hold true. For we have a love to light our path to enhance our life and it shall always help us find our way. This path of what is called discernment is one that everyone should learn to follow. Then when climbing God's mountain, the taste of becoming more alive teaches us that we are heading in the right direction. Now do you have any ideas on how we start our climb?"

"In the past, you taught me how to focus on first finding my peace. Would this be the first step?"

"At the completion of each stage of growth, every man finds himself at peace. God opens the door for us to grow up the mountain in our relations with Him every time it gets disrupted. This is how we know it is time to enter the next stage of growth on our climb. Ronan, each trial we face in life is a part of our spiritual growth and climb up the great mountain of God."

"That would mean after every trial our vision of life becomes sharper. Then the more we gain our sight from seeing even further in new heights, the view of our climb up His mountain changes with more of the light of His life."

"This is a part of discernment as well. For what you've just described are called plateau moments. In gaining perspective here, the love of God's light retrains as we no longer wish to return to the darkness of the valley of the shadow of death we've just climbed out of, but continue our growth upward into eternal life."

"So, this is what 'The valley of the shadow of death,' must refer to in its verse of situation, 'I am the vine, you are the branches and a part from me you can do nothing,' must mean! For each time we grow to reach a plateau, we reach another place of where we are seated in heavenly places with The Christ as we come out of the shadows."

"There are many who do not know how to be honest with themselves and those who live in darkness here do not know truth. For this reason they cannot find the freedom of being a friend to themselves. For they sever themselves from the vine of the living blood and the Spirit of truth that contains it."

"I see what is not seen in this spiritual world can harm you from a lack of understanding as in not seeing when it is time to grow and move on, you can remain stuck in your pain."

"You know that even when God opens a door to see to grow through, we can be held back while choosing something other than what He has for us, Ronan.

"Are you saying that we can experience the same pain over and over again by our own choices?"

"God calls us to go from glory to glory when not settling for darkness before Him. His desire is always a deeper relationship to further His light. So, do not cease to know the mercy of His grace, which empowers transformation into a love of Holy living."

"I understand. Unless we call out to The Great One in times of trouble, He will not open us to further understand our relationship with Him."

"Yet even here, He works all things for good for those who love Him 'til in each stage of growth a door is left open to move on. He uses grace to further His kingdom when losing our way without even noticing.

Now for something more immediate, Ronan. Your 4th birthday is on the morrow and I am prepared to bless you with many things. For you have won my heart. I was going to keep this a secret, but my love for you has sprouted into light and knowing how discerning you are, my joy can conceal itself no longer …"

After a big hug is felt by King Liam, his grandson continues the conversation, "I love you, grandfather!"

A wind picks up in the midst of their joy and a slight chill is felt in the air to where King Liam invites Ronan to snuggle into his blanket with him to remove the chill from His bones. A female voice is heard just after the wind dies away, "I see you two are becoming rather fond of each other," says Suzy.

Filled with excitement, Ronan looks over, "Hi, mom."

King Liam looks to his daughter, "It's been a rather long time since we've seen each other, Suzy."

"Yes, I know. What have you two been talking about that seems to have left you so joyous?"

The king speaks before Ronan can answer, "Friendship!"

Whisked Away

King Liam sits at his throne when the door slowly creaks open. Looking over, he anticipates a visit from his grandson, but a young messenger enters and delivers some news instead, "I went to summon young Ronan, but upon arrival to his home, I discovered it to be empty, King Liam."

A tear comes to the King's eye as his mouth drops open and his heart sinks. He chokes out the words, "Send for Sergeant James of the royal guard."

"Right away," is heard by the young messenger and he then departs.

Four years earlier, before Ronan had been born, an invasion took place at the lands of Dagog.

Long oars were in unison as they gently stroked the surface of the waters of the Dailey River.

A dragon head on the bow of the great ship overshadowed its currents before a waterfall was spied two hundred yards ahead. The huge red eagle crest on the center of a large bone white sail is quickly furled around its single mast. The ship glides ashore and rises upon its sands. Soon after, a hundred warriors regain their land legs while making their way down the beach of Winnies field. Passing the end of an old stone dividing wall, they further make their way into the woods of Nortica as the invasion commences.

They might have settled in the fields which were first encountered but the smell from the bog carried by the wind was foul, so they decided to keep moving. At nightfall, Cuna, their leader whistles like a bird. His brother Steel responds with a wave of his hand and leading fifty of the men onward, he proceeds towards an evening village of candlelit homes.

Cunna whistles again. The remaining men split up and a warrior named Leaf leads one group to the left while their leader moves out to the right. All draw swords and the advance continues.

However, the footprints of the hundred men have not gone unnoticed in the shine of a setting sun. Braddock and Arrow, two hunters of Nortica, were on return from their hunting earlier when they came upon them. The warriors had carelessly forgotten to cover their tracks where they disrupted the ground before entering the main trail. Recognizing the signs of a possible invasion, it is determined that Arrow would pursue on foot while Braddock went for help. Taking his extra two quivers from his horse and slinging them over his shoulder, Arrow is quick to pursue while Braddock rides for help on the open road towards Bilatz.

All at once, the man standing next to Leaf cries out in pain, then Leaf goes down himself. Five more men are next to follow and all is taken as war cries for every warrior that falls during a now dark night. This sparks forth more shouting as they run into the community, which breaks the element of surprise.

Now alerted, the villagers spring into action and go for weapons of their own. Although, Steel arrives before they can organize. There are battle clashes of sword against sword and archers are slain while going for bows in the moonlight.

In the midst of the war, a man who seems to be giving orders is noticed. Steel battles his way to him and once he has the advantage, a knife is held to King Norris's throat. He is told, "Tell your men to drop their weapons."

"Take anything you want, I only ask that you spare our lives."

"How do I know you won't retaliate?"

"Because we always treat newcomers to our province well."

"The weapons!"

"Norris cries out, "Men drop your weapons!"

Arrow stops shooting from his well concealed place back in the woods and observes all from his position at his king's command.

Cunna joins his brother Steel and holds a conference with him. While they whisper, the tension being felt by the villagers of Nortica turns to silent prayer when realizing the magnitude of what is happening. A peace falls upon Norris and his men as their trust is now in The Great One and not their situation.

Steel speaks for his brother and gives a proclamation, "Men, what do you call this place?"

King Norris answers, "Nortica."

"Men of Nortica, you are free to go."

"Go where?" asks King Norris.

"Wherever you like. However, your women will remain with us to prevent any retaliation."

The King and his men stand in disbelief for a moment 'til King Norris speaks, "Our wives and children?"

Steel senses a little fight still in them so he looks to his brother who nods, he next turns back to the king of Nortica and answers, "After a season, your wives will be released. Your daughters shall remain with us to ensure you will be neighborly. Your boys are to go with you along with your girls ten and younger."

King Norris motions with a wave of his arm and he and his men start to walk. Arrow slips away, rejoining his tribe when heading past him on a march to the Northeast country within the forest while the hunter reports to his king, "Braddock has gone for help at Bilatz. Should we regroup, your majesty?"

"Go and meet Braddock, and tell him all is well. From there you are to go to King Henry at Calington Castle and give full report, then it will be up to him to determine what to do."

"I have horse with venison and some supply at the fields between the woods, you are welcome to them."

"Arrow, we shall continue to honor the Lord by my word to the warriors. We have suffered great loss, let us not break faith with The Great One and lose our integrity as well. You are right my king, I will do what you say."

Braddock is on the road with the men from Bilatz when Arrow comes upon them and is questioned by His hunting partner, "Arrow, what happened?"

"All is well now. People of Balitz, I thank you for coming to our aide." Tension is felt in the air. When sensing they have been troubled, Arrow addresses them again, "Be sure that we will remember this for a time when you are in need."

Braddock turns and extends his arm and helps Arrow get on his horse. He starts off towards their village but his hunting partner speaks up, "First, we are to go to Calington Castle and give King Henry full report under the order of King Norris."

"That sounds rather official."

"Let us be off."

They ride on, leaving the people of Balitz behind.

Back at the village of Nortica, Steel informs his brother that Leaf and fourteen other men have been slain by shots with the same quill of many arrows. Cunna ponders to himself before responding, "A marksmen of this caliber could have easily taken us down, but why would he stop?"

"Remember, when the king gave his word …"

"…The fighting stopped! These are a people of high honor, for the man who held that bow listened to his king even though he had us at a disadvantage.

Hmmn! I do not want the woman violated, any who do so will answer to me. I want to understand this people better."

Steel salutes his brother by touching his fist to his own chest and as he turns to leave, Cunna announces, "Have Pine take Leafs place to organize a detail to bury the dead."

"Right away!" He then takes leave of his brother.

Finally, coming to a stop at the fields of Nortica after their long walk, Arrow's horse is discovered along with the deer tied to its back and tools in his saddle bag for building. With a hammer hatchet in hand and long knife, they are able to start building modest lean-tos as shelters while the children gather firewood and sticks for arrows.

King Norris has a word with his men, "Listen everyone, I know that there's a bit of a smell from the bog on the cross-breeze at times, but let it be a reminder that as we live, The Great One has not forgotten us!"

The subjects look on and nod before smiles of encouragement break-out upon their faces.

Arrow and Braddock bow their heads before King Henry at his throne.

King Henry looks on and says, "You may rise." They lift their heads and the king asks, "Now, what do you have to report?"

Arrow speaks up, "All is well by faith. Yet, there is much to tell in the way of recent events as foreign warriors have invaded our shores and have taken over our village in your land of Nortica."

Henry further inquires, "What happened?"

Braddock asks, "Yes, what did happen?"

"We were coming back from a hunt when Braddock noticed many footprints on the side of the road. Alerted to the possibility of danger, it was quickly decided that I should pursue and find out if the tracks on our path were what they seemed while Braddock went to Bilatz."

"Invaders here in our lands? What happened next?"

"Night had just fallen when I caught up to some of the warriors who were already on the advance. Concealing myself in the shadows of the trees, I let loose on them, arrow after arrow. Their death cries were mistaken for war cries going into battle under the cover of night. This is what caused the invaders to shout. This alerted the others, disrupting their element of surprise. I fired fifteen arrows towards glistening swords that were drawn and their shields which shined in the moonlight. Fifteen men then hit the ground, dying in an agonizing horror of death, for they did not know our Lord. God rest their souls."

"You seemed to have had the advantage at this point, Arrow. Whatever happened next?"

King Norris was captured and commanded us to drop our weapons, King Henry. I could not break his order, for to do so would have jeopardized all their lives."

"I understand. We shall rally the troops and free them."

"Your majesty, there is more to tell as things got strange."

"What do you mean?"

Braddock questions as well, "Yeah! What do you mean?"

"They had the men leave their weapons and had them go with the children."

"What of the women?"

Braddock questions again, "Yes. What of them?"

"They are being held to prevent anyone from retaliation."

"I will meet with them as the Lord of their land and see if they can be reasoned within a peaceable manner. You know this people, Arrow. Is a peaceable solution possible?"

"King Norris did say something about this being a possible test of the Lord, but on the other hand these warriors have no manners. Or, perhaps it is too soon to tell."

King Henry gives his advise, "You two will remain here as I can tell by the tone of your voice this is still too personal for you."

Arrow protests, "Doth King Norris not be your friend make this personable for you as well?"

"What would you suggest?"

"I can stand guard with an arrow in hand from off in the distance if you permit. This would over-rule my king's order to stand down and make me most effective in your service …"

Braddock steps forward and puts his arm around his shoulder, " …and with me by his side looking after him, what could go wrong?"

"I will check with my advisor, too. Be on the ready as he has been sent for."

"The beloved healer enters from by the doorway of the king's court, "You sent for me, your majesty."

"How much of our conversation have you overheard?"

"Enough to know that you should send an envoy to check the condition of the woman first. If they have not been disrespected, your visit should be announced forthcoming as a peaceful one if they release the queen to you as a token of good faith. Otherwise, they should anticipate a reprisal for upsetting the tenants of your lands. It then must be acknowledged that a peaceful resolution is less costly than war. A single arrow should then be fired from a well-concealed place. The quill of your arrow will be recognized as fired under a now higher authority because you are no longer beholden to your king, Arrow."

"Would you be my envoy, most noble healer?" says King Henry.

"I will consider it a high honor to be your voice on this matter."

"Choose two champions to go with you in full armor as a show of what we are capable of."

"I see that you have good counsel, too. Thank you, old friend."

A concerned looking King Norris is in prayer when his teen nephew, Hunter, comes upon him, "You sent for me, uncle?"

"The moment seems to have swallowed me, but now my focus has returned to the answer of your voice."

Forgive my impatience, uncle, I thought you were asleep and did not realize you were in conversation."

"Oh, the impetuousness of youth. We are always at prayer, yet not always mindful of what we are mindful of. For what is dim has so many shades of dark 'til one completely embraces the light to find full satisfaction in life."

"I do not understand what you are saying, uncle."

"I had to lose everything to start over and rekindle my relationship with the giver of life. This may sound odd, nephew, but those warriors may have actually been sent by The Great One to bring me to where I am now. For I am grateful to be with Him again."

"Why are you telling me this, uncle?"

"Because, I have not been a good enough example within my life, for you have been walking in the shadows and not the light.

Come here my boy as I need to ask for your forgiveness because now I am capable of loving more."

His nephew then asks, "You were never there when I needed you most."

"Love never fails, try me." The king extends his hand.

"I'll consider what you say, uncle."

"As The Great One says from the cross, 'Forgive them Father for they know not what they do' re-enters my mind, I see how blind I was by light. Oh, how I walked away through night, until by grace I regained my sight. Will you sit with me at supper?"

"All right, I will."

"Remember, this is a time for us all to start over."

"Thanks for the advice. I shall see you at sup."

Arrow and Braddock are well concealed behind some trees.

There is an arrow in his bow and Braddock stands on the ready with battle-ax in hand. The healer and two riders are on well armed horses. Knights ride with their helmets down to appear even more menacing as they enter the village of Nortica while bearing a white flag.

Passing the guard warriors, they are seen on the main street and Cunna is summoned in his hut by steel, "We have a situation that is in need of your attention."

Cunna rises, exits the hut behind Steel, and they soon find themselves standing in front of the healer. He is still mounted next to the men on armed horses.

The healer looks at the men standing before him. Then enquiring of Cunna, "You would be the leader?"

"Yes, how did you know?"

"The truth of The Great One reveals all."

"Great One?"

"Stick around our provinces long enough and you shall soon learn that He is a friend to all."

"Your provinces?" Cunna's eyes rest upon his armed accompaniment.

"However, because you are new to this land and did not know that these land's belonged to Henry Calington of Calington Castle, he is willing to overlook this incident of evicting his tenants."

Steel steps in between them and becomes involved, "We took this land …"

An arrow sings through the air and comes to a rest before his feet and the healer tells all, "Another move like that and you will be buried here in this land. Although, know it well! Because we have come in peace, you still live. Now, you are to release Queen Shirley as a sign of good faith and the king will meet with you to deliver terms of peace. Know it now as a servant of the Great one, he shall be very fair."

A look of concern meets with Cunna's face when he sees the feathers of the arrow. He then goes over, picks it up, and holding it before his face makes a comment, "The grey quill of a morning dove. This is the same quill that was found in our men after last eve's battle."

"I see that you're familiar with our champion archer's arrow."

"Where would he be?" says Steel.

"Oh, you'll meet him or his arrow soon enough."

Cunna holds his hand up to his chin and pauses for a moment before his reply, "Fetch the queen."

Steel protests, "You back down to a single arrow?"

"You will remain silent! Pine, fetch the queen."

Pine honors Cunna by touching his fist to his chest and saying, "At once!"

Steel approaches his brother in a sulky way, "You know my heart is for our people."

"Is it?"

How can you question?"

"Your heart is for yourself now." Cunna turns his back on steel as a hardness grips his heart.

There is silence between the two brothers while the queen is brought before them.

"Queen Shirley's face lights with delight when she sees the healer with his accompaniment. The healer comments, "It is good to see you well, Shirley."

"Yes, I am well."

The healer extends his arm to the queen who first looks to Cunna for permission and he responds by saying, "You are free to go."

Walking between the two silent brothers, she takes the healers hand and mounts his horse. Next, they all turn and go their way.

Steel and Cunna are left looking on each other in silence while being left behind.

The Great Rebellion of Past

In the shadows of a temple, a warrior stands facing the back of the high priest, "Well Pine, you have always been good at handling things in secret for me."

"What is it that you require of me?"

"A ship awaits with a remnant of our choice warriors, be on it. For should my sons fail me, you will be required to carry on our tradition of the Elder's. So, keep watch as usual and you will know what to do when the time is right with the knife I have given you. For the hand which will grip the handle of this knife will do what is required to preserve our heritage by carrying out all of our ancestral spirits' requests. Now go to the ship out the back as usual. Make sure you are not seen and await for Cunna to come to the ship.

In the far away land of Ducil, another meeting follows swiftly which takes place between Eridu and his son at an altar dedicated to the horned statue of Nimrod where blood is being poured out over a silver jewel handled knife. The blood enters into the knife and the father picks up the knife and inserts it into a slot in the heart of the statue. The statue dissolves and turns into a green mist until only the knife remains. The father picks up the knife from the altar and tells his son to kneel before handing it to him. Cunna's face is revealed as he raises his head from out of the shadows and looks to his father for instruction, "Cunna, this knife will show you favor, but it is also a weapon with the power to grant your brother immortality. One day he will rise up against you and then you must decide to die and break the chain of succession of our god's or pass your brother's spirit beyond the veil of darkness.

You will continually hear from him, for your bond shall remain the same in the spirit world. In this way, there would be no more threat of bodily harm between the two of you. For there is a chance, if you fought each other, both of you would die."

"I would have to murder Steel, my own brother?"

"I have prepared a ship with a hundred of our bravest warriors. You must find a new land and settle there, go now for there is not much time."

"Why don't you come with us, father?"

"The enemy is coming for me, I must remain to maintain order as a diversion for your escape. I have been advised by the spirit world that I cannot win. You must go!"

"I will remember you, father."

"It is more important that you remember your heritage."

"When the time comes, I will do this."

"The time for you to leave is now. Your brother is already on the ship with provision. Go!"

Eridu turns his back on his son and Cunna leaves.

Back at the village of Nortica, Pine is listening to Steel who is talking, "I have lost face before my brother and it is more than I can bear, Pine."

"I know a way you can regain favor with Him."

"How?"

"From the meeting that we had earlier, it looks like your brother wants to make peace with King Henry. We are warriors and will always be warriors as it is in our nature to fight."

"I cannot go against my brother, what are you suggesting?"

"No, not going against your brother, but to surprise him by holding to our traditions as warriors."

"What is your plan?"

Now back at the castle, Queen Shirley of Nortica stands next to the healer and before King Henry at his throne, "It is good to see you again, Henry …"

" …and you Shirley, now what doth your intuition tell you about our conquering warriors? Cunna, their leader holds all in order. He seems a just man and can be trusted to deal with."

"Very good. Queen Shirley, I trust your judgement."

"Do you have anything you wish to add, old friend?"

"I agree with Queen Shirley, though his brother is rash and unpredictable. And then there is the possibility of others like him. How do we know if there are not more to come? I feel it be best if this matter were resolved quickly while there is yet time to befriend, show him homages, and earn his favor. Then if others should come, there are advantages of having friends in the right places. For would this not assure peace?"

"You forget about the character of The Great One, my wise natured old friend. We honor Him first. However, your counsel is in line with the essence of His Spirit and will be taken, you've done well most noble healer.

Liam enters with his daughter who leaves his side and goes to King Henry, giving him a hug. He laughs with the warmth of his heart and hands her a gold bracelet which she admires while walking away. Liam then questions, "What was the advice your old friend was giving you this time?"

"Liam, I know it has been difficult for you since Ashley has gone to stay with her uncle and aid him in his old age. I still feel it best, you tend to Suzy."

"Perhaps, most noble healer, you can tell me what's going on?"

"What? And go against the adventure of your father running the kingdom in his glory days? You're asking the wrong man."

"Very well, father …'

"Liam, she grows faster than imagined. She needs your wisdom."

"Perhaps you are right father."

"Liam, I am going out on what I hope will be my last, great adventure as I am getting old. You will rule in my absence temporarily."

"When will you be leaving so I can make arrangements for Ashley to return?"

Queen Shirley makes a suggestion, "I will be here a few days. Perhaps I could be of some assistance by just being a concerned ear?"

"I will be leaving on the morrow at morn, Liam."

"Well, it looks like The Great One's hand has moved again.

Thank you, Queen Shirley. Your help is most welcome."

Out on the fields of Nortica, two wagons filled with supply reach the fields. King Norris, welcomingly meets Arrow who drives the lead wagon. "I thought I'd find you here, majesty."

Braddock pulls his wagon next to Arrow's, "What's that I smell? Fresh venison roasting on an open fire?"

"Care to join us for supper? I'm sure my nephew will be glad that you are joining us as well."

The other men from the village unload some of the supply to add to the meal. Arrow notices and makes a proclamation, "Tonight we feast!"

The sun shines ten o'clock in the morn as the king and his accompaniment enter the village of Nortica.

Pine summons Cunna. He rises and throws some water on his face from a basin and shakes off his sleep while exiting his hut. He appears before King Henry and notices that his brother is nowhere in sight, which he dismisses because of their disagreement that he had during the prior visit by the healer. Looking back to the king, he bows his head, "Majesty."

"Cunna, look on me." He raises his head, looks at Henry, and asks, "What are your terms?"

"You do not understand as they are not my terms but the High King's."

"I thought that you were the High King?"

"Of Calington, I am king, but not over heaven and earth."

"You speak to me in a riddle."

"In time, you will find that all answers lead to The Great One as He is the High King that all who seek to be just serve."

"Our god says that one must fight and rule with strength. Justice is in the sword!"

"The Great One, the God of all, says that peace is strength."

"I do not understand."

"War is like a storm at sea that strikes the rock and is broken 'til there is the peace of calm."

"You intrigue me, King Henry."

"When making peace with the Creator of heaven and earth, what shall man be that one should be mindful of him when the trust of every heart lay in having peace with Him?"

"Very well spoken, but enough for now as you have given me much to consider."

"Now, here are my terms." The leader of the warriors gives Henry his full attention. "Cunna, you and your men shall come and live among us to learn of our ways, then we'll talk of a land that you and your people can settle in where you will have a land of your own."

"I am sorry for the lives I have taken from my lack of understanding. You are wiser than I."

"There is no need for apology. For when it is of what pride demands, it clangs like a cymbal in the wind, but love as forgiveness is always the better choice."

Cunna walks over and falls upon King Henry's leg as he sits upon his horse and unburdens his heart while sobbing, "Thank you for your mercy."

King Henry places his hand on his head in empathy and says, "I know you have suffered much …and as for wisdom, you shall soon learn that it comes from God. For the Spirit of His wisdom speaks through me even now and I am humbled by it."

All men look on as Cunna lifts his head and looks on through his tears, "Thank you."

"You are going to like my sons. You shall meet them when you come to live with me."

A new found joy appears as a smile on his face as he expresses himself, "I look forward to it."

In the fields of Nortica, Braddock awakes and uncovering himself, he notices the position of the sun. He then rouses Arrow in urgency, "I believe we have overslept as King Henry is to meet with Cunna today."

Arrow rolls over to go back to sleep, saying, "The Great One will watch over him."

"…But doth it not rain on the just and the unjust?"

Arrow sits up and says while getting himself together, "You are right. Let us be off!"

Gathering themselves, Arrow picks up his bow and quiver filled with arrows and hands Braddock his battle-axe as he is already sitting on his horse. He then mounts up and leaving the encampment, the two start on their way. Exiting the fields, they ride hard on the main road til reaching the turn off to the village of Nortica. Tears suddenly meet with their eyes when coming across the bodies of their fallen king and his accompaniment.

Braddock looks on and shouts, "They've taken our majesty's head!"

A basket is carried into the village of Nortica. Steel holds it in his hand while approaching his brother who seems rather pleased. "You look pleased, Cunna. Yet, I have even better news for you here in this basket." Removing the cover he entreats his brother to look in the basket, "Behold, the head of our oppressor. Now we shall possess the land!"

Cunna cries out, "You have killed a lion-lamb!"

"You are not pleased, brother, that I have upheld the code of the warriors?"

"I would rather join King Henry than stay here with you."

"Steel looks on Pine, "Pine gave me the idea!"

Pine shrugs his shoulders, "I am in allegiance with you and know nothing of this. I even swear on the integrity of King Henry's last word's to you." Crossing his fingers behind his back he signifies to the spirit world that lies and truth can exist together.

"He lies, brother!"

Cunna takes a breath in the midst of his grief, "I have something I want to show you in the way of inheritance. I believe that now is the time for you to receive it. Come with me to the hut."

The two brothers turn and head for the hut. Steel follows behind until they enter.

"You will have my words of counsel, but first I must tell you that King Henry was a just man that has two sons which I am sure will behave just like their father."

"Sons? What shall we do?"

Cunna goes and fetches his father's knife. "This was left for us, but I want no part of it now because of the wisdom King Henry has imparted to me before you took off his head!"

"The knife is beautiful!"

"Not as beautiful as the words of the kings life you just took. So, now you must listen to the lesson you wil learn and know why I am leaving the next choice up to you."

"What are you talking about?"

"There is a story that goes along with the knife that I used to believe had value."

"What was it, brother?"

"For the sake of King Henry's honor that all must learn from, father said, 'I would have to make a choice over who would die between you and I.' For if we fought each other, he feared that both of us would die."

"Why are you telling me this?"

"Wait! There is more. He said if you were to die by this knife that I would still be able to communicate with you from beyond the other side. I have the choice of ending our ancestry or if I let you kill me, you shall continue it on. I can no longer make this choice, so I will let you rule over this decision in my place." Cunna turns his back on his brother and says, "Here, I have made it easy for you, unless you decide to come and meet King Henry's sons and live in peace."

"I would rather die a warriors death and honor the god of our ancestors as the price of war is more glorious to me than living in peace." Steel hold's the knife up to his heart and falling forward on the blade impales himself.

Cunna cries, "Nooo! What have you done? The battle for inner peace is the more glorious one. For the true war lies within oneself." He turns his brother and holds him in his arms.

"It is too late, brother. For, I can see the door of a blackness opening unto me. It calls for me to leave my body as even now I understand that I have an eternal soul. It enters into darkness unless guided by the light I see from far away off in the distance. I guess I will be talking to you from the other side like you spoke. It's so cold and it's getting so dark." Steel dies in his brother's arms and Cunna begins to weep.

While the leader joins the others, Pine looks on Cunna, as he approaches with a blank and morbid stare, "Pine, you shall be the new magistrate that will rule in my brother's place."

"Where is Steel?"

"He chose to leave us."

"Where did he go?"

"He has taken his own life."

"Curse this land and the lineage of King Henry. We never should have landed here or anywhere, but remained with your father and fought to the death by your brother's side as I loved him and what we once stood for."

"Death is cold and dark from what I understand and there is no glory in it. I am telling you this so you'll understand that never could you have loved him more than me, for the depth of our bond understood what it was to be ourselves in acknowledging each other since youth!"

Pine realizes how vulnerable Cunna now is and suggests, "Let us both live on for Steel together then."

"When the time comes, you shall serve the magistrate over our new province well."

"I suppose after the counsel I gave, I will at that …Where are you going?"

"We must go to Calington, for that was king Henry's last command."

"This is not our way as we are warriors."

Cunna draws his sword and Pine is quick to use his tongue, "You cannot kill me because you have just appointed me magistrate. This goes against our code!"

Returning his sword to his shield, the leader looks on with fire in his eyes.

"Now that we understand each other, I will inform the men."

Arrival at the Castle

Cunna rides a horse that draws a wagon with a white flag of surrender tied to it. He is at the head of his men as they approach Calington Castle. An arrow suddenly sings out and strikes the ground before the horse he rides. Rising up on its hind legs, its rider steadies it 'til it becomes calm again. The healer and Arrow observe all from up on the wall above the gates. The leader of the warriors dismounts and lays down his weapons. His men follow him in doing so and before long the remainder of his men have stacked a pile three feet high.

In observance of the arms being laid down and the white flag, Braddock rides from the castle towards the encampment of his people.

Cunna smacks the horse forward and the men follow along until a second arrow is launched and strikes the ground. Cunna stops and kneels and hangs his head and his other men follow suit.

As the horse proceeds onward, the body of his brother and a basket with the king's crown upon it slowly comes into view 'til it is fully discovered by the guards at the gate. One of the guards enters the castle and returns with a now King Liam, along with priests Louis and Andre. Louis lifts the crown and says, "Under the authority of The Great One, I place this crown upon your head. May He bless you with wisdom, compassion and mercy from His heights."

Andre lifts the basket after the crown has been lowered and starts to take it inside the castle while bowing his head. Liam asks him to wait and all pause while he rests his hand upon the basket. A slight tremor is felt upon the ground and the earth quakes. Tears fill Liam's eyes as he looks towards heaven and says, "Thank you for Your love, my King." He then nods and Andre proceeds to bring the basket inside to where Queen Mary, standing just inside, touches the basket while Prince Edward steadies her.

King Liam waves at Cunna to address him. He next comes forward and meets the king of Calington. "The healer told me that this body once belonged to your brother. How did he die?"

"I told him that I would rather be with your father whom he murdered more than him. For I knew the beauty that dwelt in Henry Calington, your father. When I told him this and that he should turn himself over to his kin, which would be you, he refused. He said that he would rather die a warriors death than die in peace and then he took his own life while I was there before I could do anything."

"It's not your falt as not everyone can handle transition from darkness to light, for most fear what they do not understand. They've been conditioned to believe what they already have is best. You may now take his body and bury it."

"We have no land to call our own. Where am I to bury him?"

King Liam responds, "Then he will be buried here on Calington soil as a sign of transition for you and all men. A memorial will be set for him outside the gate."

"Your father's last word's to me were that I would enjoy meeting you and your brother."

"Wearing the crown of my father helps me to see things clearly. I am King Liam and yonder is Queen Shirley whom you already know. By her side is my daughter, Princess Suzy, and brother Prince Edward. We both had losses. I, my father and you your brother. We both suffer, that is enough for now as the loss of our loved ones have created tears within our hearts and they need time to heal."

"Me and my men grieve my brother as you do your father, but we must remember it is harder for us as we are still here in this realm." He next responds to his fallen brother, Steel, who has whispered a thought into his mind from out of the dimness of the dimension of where he finds himself. "…What was that you said?"

"I said to ask him where he got all his light, for in him I see no darkness."

"What was what?" asks King Liam.

"My brother says that you have much light in you and asks how he can get it. In order to join the light, he sees from a longways off within his dark place?"

"I am sorry. For now my heart beckons me in another direction as I am in much grief, but at another time I will hear more on this matter."

"Then there is hope?"

"Yes, there is always hope."

Steel speaks again, "The light from off in the distance just got a little brighter. Ask him what he hopes in."

"My brother says that he has more light already."

When Cunna turns, he sees that Liam has already turned away. He has gone over to hug his brother who sobs and then they cry together. Queen Shirley then rises and hugs them both.

The healer walks from the gate and arriving by their leader, he gives him a hug and says, "I am sorry about the loss of your brother …" Cunna hugs him back and as they comfort each other, he says, "… And I for the loss of your king."

Breaking from their hug the healer suggests, "Accommodations of tent and food shall be brought for you and your men. However, after your men are settled and your weapons put away, you will return to the castle to familiarize yourself with the grounds while staying with us."

Cunna replies, "I understand."

King Norris is making a clearing with his men at the edge of the forest with a community of lean-tos that lean up against some of the larger trees nearby. Braddock rides up to him and delivers a message, "Your majesty, we can all return to our village as the warriors have left."

The king in response shouts, "Did you hear that everybody? We are going home!"

There are shouts of joy and excitement is in the air 'til the king notices the somber look on the face of Braddock. There is a sudden silence that causes everyone else to quiet down as they all look at him and realize there is more to the message. As all eyes are resting upon Braddock who responds, "King Henry is dead. Long live, King Liam."

A sort of hysteria is in the air as the people are stuck between crying and rejoicing at the same time. King Noris speaks for everyone as he becomes their voice, "I weep for King Henry who has been not only a friend to me but to us all. Let us remember him as we load the wagons he has provided as Braddock returns to the village to fetch us our horses." He looks to one of his men and says, "Devin, you're good with horses. I am sure you would like to go with him and help."

Braddock lowers his arm and helps him mount while the rest of the men somberly begin to load the wagons. Devin holds onto Braddock as they start on their way.

Cunna looks from a window in the courtyard and takes in the view. He is able to see just over the castle wall where he gets a glimpse of his men who are finishing up the tents they're building.

After finishing their encampment out on the field, Pine expresses himself to the men, "It appears as though Cunna has abandoned our ways and perhaps even us."

Gray, one of the men, stands in opposition and defends their leader, "He just lost his brother and is not fully himself. Give him a chance to get past this. He'll probably come to us in a few days …"

"…And if he doth not?"

Grey ponders before he speaks, "Then he would probably have good cause."

Another meeting is taking place in the castle between the healer, Prince Edward, and King Liam in his chamber.

Edward is summarizing what has just been discussed, "So, you are saying that it will be more effective for Cunna to be separated from his tribe during the training for him to learn our art of wisdom?"

King Liam shares his thoughts, "Yes, it will be necessary while our knowledge is applied to his life. For he might continue to be locked into the pattern of his men, otherwise."

His brother responds, "I agree with this, but if you want me to look after him in this matter, I feel he must be a part of the process of how the new province shall be established in the North West fields of Nortica, too."

The healer shares a thought, "Just him coming here is all the answer we need. For if he learns truth without patient love to balance him out, he'll become prideful and want to rebel. Your father must have left quite an impression on him to have come here the way he did."

Prince Edward responds, "I feel it would give him more incentive to learn if he knew that a province was being established for him and his men after his training was complete. Why, he could even name the province."

After taking in some more of their counsel, King Liam becomes involved again, "I feel letting Cunna name the province is an excellent idea when the time comes, but for now we must be cautious not to lose focus as to what true freedom really is. For unless he fully embraces The Great One's light to come out of the dark, history may repeat itself until it is too late for him to awaken. As we all know, a mind that is awake cannot go back to sleep. The love of this truth always restrains once experiencing the independence of having a peace that will not want to be lost. Our healer is right. He may become anxious about his men and become distracted from the embrace of wanting to maintain his peace. This might cause him to want to leave us prematurely and stunt his growth of wisdom."

"Brother, perhaps if we split up his men into two groups so that he would not know the project was underway he would remain at peace about the whole idea and be more focused on learning our practices."

Edward, at eve you shall start going over plans with him for how he'd want His province laid out. Then once it was completed, we could have his men build it. Half the men shall remain here and every other week, we could swap work forces and keep the men working and rested."

The healer interjects "…Then while he is with us, should he look upon his men he'll not realize any men have left. It is a good plan, but what if he notices some of his men are missing?"

Prince Edward comments, "We could tell Cunna that the men are on training drills and are learning different things so that when they come back together, they'll have the adventure of learning from each other to keep our new practices fresh in mind."

King Liam's eyes light with a smile, "That would work!"

Cunna is looking towards his men out of a window when a knock is heard at the door and answers, "Who is it?"

"It is Prince Edward. Would you like some company?"

He walks over and opens the door to the prince and says while looking at him, "Company is welcome."

"Is your room satisfactory?"

"It is different than what I'm used to."

"What have you learned since you've been here?"

"For one, I have learned that I miss my men."

"Keep in mind that you are here for their good. This will make your transition from darkness unto understanding the light of our ways a little easier as it is a journey."

"I have led my people well."

"From what you understand, you have. Yet, how many men have you lost since you've come to this land?"

"Leadership comes with a price. Why do you question me?"

"Asking questions is a part of learning. Ask yourself, 'Was there a way you could have entered our lands without losing any of your men needlessly?'"

"Perhaps."

"I see that pride dies hard."

"Agreed."

"You may not be aware of it but this room is a part of your training."

"What do you mean?"

"First, you must arrive here to fully take in the view of your new surroundings as your mind is still out there on the field with your men."

"I have walked in your castle already."

"But how did you walk?"

"With my feet of course."

"No, what was your attitude while you walked?"

"To learn where I am."

"Now, could you learn about this castle if you kept looking at your men?"

"What is your point?"

"Your mind is your castle and when you have thoughts that distract you from having clarity, it is like walking into a wall continually. So, until you can see the attitudes behind your actions, you cannot go through the necessary changes for a complete transition in your life."

"You speak of change after a lifetime of knowing my men and my men knowing me. I enjoy my comrade in arms. Why should this change?"

"Why did you come here?"

Cunna remains silent and doth not speak.

"Your silence smells of pride because you came here to seek our wisdom. Now, so you'll know from this time forth, the price of our wisdom is your very life. For after you go through your transformation, you will find the wisdom that you seek will change the very nature of it."

Steel's voice is heard within Cunna's mind and he flinches, *"If you do not humble yourself, brother, then I will never get out of this dimly lit place I am in!"*

Cunna answers Prince Edward, "You are right, I was being prideful, though not only for myself but the heritage of my people who seem to be in a dark place compared to your light."

"Humbling oneself is the beginning of transformation as it was the same for me, Cunna." He extends his hand and when the leader of the warriors takes it, they shake with a firm grip."

"I feel as though I stand at the door to a new way of life."

"Not only for you, but for all your people as you'll have a light that will shine brighter than what you now have."

"I understand."

"I too am in need of understanding. I must know of you and your people. For whether you are aware of it or not, you carry a great deal of information. Tell me what was your old village like."

"This land no longer exists."

"As long as it exists in your memory it lives."

"Why do you persist in knowing?"

"We are in the process of picking out a separate province for you and your men."

"Why would you do this?"

"Because our God of true light is from true light and is a rewarder of those who diligently seek the truth of Him."

"What is the name of your God?"

"The Great One, and in time He will reveal himself to you. For He is in the essence of the nature of all created things."

"How is this possible?"

"Before being born, the all of everything is with the One who says of Himself, I Am."

"Then He knew me before I was in my mother's womb!"

"By the power of the light of this truth, you are correct."

"Steel speaks to the mind of Cunna again, *"Ask him about the light of truth, for the darkness has faded a little more."*

"I will be straight with you. My brother, Steel, suffers in a dark realm while standing by the entrance to a door within the thoughts of my mind."

"Are you sure that you're not keeping him alive in your memory?"

"Ever since he fell on an accursed knife, I can hear him audibly."

"I have heard of accursed knives from King Liam. Though, I have never experienced this situation myself. As my brother still grieves right now, come with me to our priests at their rectory as they have more knowledge about these knives than I."

"What is a rectory?"

"It is a place where they live, now come."

The priests are just pouring some vegetables into a pot that hangs from a chain over an open flame when a knock is heard at the door.

Louis inquires, "Who's there?"

"Prince Edward, 'I am here with, Cunna.'"

Louis calls to Andre before opening the door, "Set out two more bowls. It looks like we're having some company for sup this eve."

As he opens the door to their guests, Prince Edward says while overhearing, "Nevermind about sup. We have a problem that needs your attention." Andre puts the extra bowls away and joins them as Prince Edward turns to Cunna and says, "Repeat to them what you told me concerning your brother."

Looking to the priests he shares what is on his heart, "My brother communes with me in my thoughts with his voice while in a dark place. He says that from off in the distance he sees a light. I beg of you to have mercy on us as I have heard, you have handled this problem with Liam before he was a king."

Andre shares what he knows, "I was with Liam when such a case happened before. Tell me, was there anything like an amulet involved?"

Cunna is puzzled and asks, "What is an amulet?"

Prince Edward interjects, "There was a knife and the light seems to get brighter every time the truth of The Great One is mentioned."

"My brother just told me, *'That is right!'*"

Andre continues his questioning, "Do you or did your brother know The Great One before he died?"

"I know of the Great One, but do not know him in the way I have heard you describe."

"Alright, this is what must be done. First, for your's and your brother's sake, you must receive the Spirit of our living Lord to be reunited with Him and complete the cycle of creation. This will make you both His bride and prepare you to receive the gift of eternal life. Next, as a dead bloodline has no heritage of life, you must receive the living flesh and regenerative blood of the resurrection to grant you both eternal life. For as your brother is joined to you, he shall receive it, too. But before this happens you must renounce your heritage of what ties you to this world. The knife must be destroyed and its ancestry renounced while doing so."

"I have many questions."

"First, hand over the knife."

"But I do not have it."

Prince Edward volunteers, "Where is the knife? Perhaps I can retrieve it while Louis and Andre answer your questions and instruct you further."

Louis and Andre step away and whisper for a few moments and upon returning, say together, "Agreed!"

Prince Edward further enquires, "Now, where is the knife?"

"Pine, my magistrate has it out in the camp before the castle, but he'll not surrender it easy as he is fond of our heritage and was close to my brother. It is all he has to remember him by."

Prince Edward takes leave while Cunna begins to ask questions of the priests, "So where exactly is my brother that I may understand how he is to be freed?"

Louis answers, "His soul is being refined by the truth of purging fire, this is why darkness leaves him. For as more of the truth is dispensed from the living words of *The Book of Life,* they give off our Lord's light."

"What is this *Book of Life*?"

"They are living words of light from The Great One's purity of Spirit which point to the root of the holy tree of life."

Andre becomes involved and continues to answer Cunna's question, "Once you enter into relations with Him by receiving His seed of living flesh and blood, you become married to Him and enter His family by completing the cycle of eternal life."

"I do not fully understand."

"You will by the time we finish educating you. Just know for now that once you cross over from dimness of mind to bright, you shall remain in brilliance with your brother and you shall both encounter the clothing of Holy Spirit light."

Louis expounds, "You shall be in this world and no longer of it as you both are being translated into having prepared glorified bodies that will never wear out. This is a part of growing from this world to being seated in the peace of the heavenly place of the other, which you'll now be able to experience while here on earth. For you'll have an eternal life that will place you in three stages of being at the same time. As you will be in a stage of being translated, from out of your past and into the moment while knowing where you are going. Our word for all three stages of growth at the same time is a Hebrew word called, Shalom. For, *The Book of Life* says, that we are saved, being saved, and are already saved to back up this claim."

Wow! This is all so fantastic.

Andre becomes involved again, "The Great One's Spirit has just told me that only a three-fold cord of light will allow your brother to climb up to the purity of God's throne."

"How would this happen?"

This will happen by you being planted in eternal life by entering into a relationship with Him. Then reaching back to help your brother up into the eternal kingdom through your growth within the light and by us praying for his soul at the same time, he shall receive all that is promised by the Christ."

"What exactly do you mean by eternal life?"

Andre looks to Louis who gestures with his hand as if to say, go ahead and tell him. So Andre continues, "We are crafted as the crown of all God's creation, but unlike animals and plants which have come together within us, we were given a living soul that lasts forever. Eternal life happens when we get planted into our glorified bodies by what is called the free gift of grace. It is free because, The Great One, being our creator wants to reconnect with his children out of love. Your brother has been given an exceptional gift. For he knows that it is better to choose the gift of light of God's living love over being condemned to an eternal death of living in the confusion of darkness here on earth first hand."

"I was just taught that eternal life was the place that we went to live forever to be with our ancestors after this life. I never knew that we could be planted here on earth to have an eternal walk while in the coolness of dark as well."

"All this will be clearly established as you are trained from the notes of our Monsignor while you are with us. Then you will be able to read from *The Book of Life* with understanding. For it can be a stumbling block to those who trust they know what they read by spirits of pride. These are the ones who wrestle its verse to their own destruction without vision beyond the dark and remain discontent while searching them for life. So, put everything out of your mind that you'll be ready to learn or you may end up in the dark."

Cunna looks to the priest with enthusiasm, "I am ready!"

Battle Against the Spirit

"Would you be Pine?"

"…and the magistrate. Who's asking?"

"I am Prince Edward from Calington Castle at your service."

"How do I know that you are really him?"

"You can tell by my manner of dress for one."

"At you service ay, you say. Get down on your knees and bark like a dog."

"Why are you being so difficult when I am here to help?"

"I don't need your help. For, I have this lovely tent village to live in."

"I have come to change these living conditions, which we will talk about."

"Talk! Did you hear that everyone!" A crowd starts to gather around the two of them.

Prince Edward sizing up the situation speaks with wisdom, "I have come in Cunna's name and represent him. So, I expect the same respect that you would give him."

Pine then changes his tone in front of the men and says, "I was just having a little fun, tis all as there ain't much to do around here."

Prince Edward becomes enthused, "Right now, everything is changing. It is being worked out how all of you are going to be put to work building a province for yourselves."

A hardy shot of, "Ho!" Fills the air as arms go up with a fist.

Pine then asks, "If it has been worked out already then why have you come?"

"I was sent to fetch the knife that Steel took his own life with."

"Then you are a dog! If you'd believe that I would give it up for any reason, you are mistaken."

"It has taken me a long time to find you already. Although, Cunna did say you'd be difficult about handing it over to me."

"How do I know that you didn't overhear what you're telling me and are trying to get me to play the fool?"

"Because I knew to come to you and ask for it."

"It will not leave my hand, unless I hand it over to Cunna, personally!"

"I can assure you that he is in need of it."

"Yah, hear that everyone? You are all my witnesses. That alone would suffice if it were not for the fact it is worth more to me than my very own life."

"If that be the case, you may as well come along and hand it to him as I do not enjoy killing, personally."

Pine suggests, "Come on, I want to see how my leader is doing."

The two start to walk towards the castle gate.

Back at the rectory, Cunna's eyes are filled with brilliance of light as he expresses what is on his heart, "The notes of your monsignor have really moved me with great understanding from all you have read."

"Knock, knock! Knock, knock, knock!" Is heard at the door.

"That's a new knock," says Andre.

"Yes, very unusual!" answers Louis.

"That would be our magistrate, Pine," says Cunna. "I knew that he would not let the knife leave his sight."

He next hears the voice of his brother impressed upon his mind, *"It is sad, how he cleaves so deeply to the thoughts of what is dark. It's going to be hard for him to receive any light. So, my counsel to you is to get rid of him quick that he'll not interfere with the destruction of the knife."*

Cunna quickly steps in front of the priests and half way opens the door. The leader questions his magistrate, "I heard your knock, Pine. How are the men?"

"They grow restless."

"Do you have the knife?"

"Yes, what's this all about?"

"May I have it please?"

Pine hands over the knife while asking, "Can I come in?" He tries to peek inside.

"I need you to return to the men and keep order. I will explain all else later." Closing the door, he turns facing the priests. Then Louis asks, "Weren't you a little abrupt with him?"

"I know my men."

Pine stands looking at the door 'til he hears Prince Edwards voice, "Shall we return to the other men?"

"What are you doing to him that he'd close a door on me?"

"We're turning your leader into a king, for the good of all men ..."

Pine answers while staring at the closed door, "...Let us return to the field."

In the rectory, Cunna stands beholding the knife in his hand, "It looks so majestic!"

Louis answers, "You are being seduced by the spirits connected with it."

"How shall I destroy it?"

Andre volunteers, "I believe it may add to the flavor of my vegetable soup from beneath the pot in the flame."

Louis announces, "I would so like to hear a renouncing of it while you placed it in the fire."

Cunna nods before asking, "Doth The Great One go by another name that I may renounce it under His authority of light to defeat the darkness of this blade?"

Andre states, "You've learned your lessons of what's been taught well in such a short time as the spirits of that knife will be defeated by the High King's light under the authority of the name of Jesus, The Christ."

Cunna replies while walking to the flame, "By the name of the High King Jesus Christ, I renounce my heritage connected with this knife." He then quickly shoves it within the flames before him.

"Glorious!" Shouts Andre.

"Glory indeed! As my brother has said, *I've the warmth of love within my heart and more light in my sight."* He has impressed this within my thoughts.

"Though I have light and warmth, it is still dark around me."

"My brother has just spoken to me again about having warmth of light and yet still being surrounded by darkness.

Louis looks at Cunna and says, "Those who know the truth have inner peace, for once the truth grows to eat up what is dark, a life becomes trimmed of its shadows to walk in light, a light that knows that truth contains life."

Cunna asks, "How shall my brother know this light of life?"

Louis answers, "As long as you walk in the light, you will keep the truth that knows life for both your brother Steel and you. Because you've renounced your heritage in the name of Christ, you've opened the door for many others to find brilliance this day, too.

"How did this happen?"

"You chose the person of truth to replace the liar. Remember, if you've looked to the stars in the night sky, you will notice they always shine brighter. Truth is as such for one who walks in the light."

"Then is my brother now as one in the night sky?"

"He has started his dance but has not yet ascended to his proper place in heaven."

"What can be done?"

"You must ask The Great one to intercede for him on his behalf."

"For how long?"

"Til you can hear his voice from a long way off and then no more. At that time, you will know that he has joined the light beyond the sky 'til night shines within the brilliant city by The King on High."

"Lord, if my brother would have had more time to know you better before his passing, I am sure he would have served you well as it was becoming to his character even though he was misdirected. You know his heart. Allow him Your grace to have passage to your kingdom, Amen."

"Steel has impressed upon my mind that there is more light, but as things are a little hazy more prayer is needed."

"I understand. I will pray with you says Andre and Louis." The priests walk over and place their hands on his shoulder.

"What are you doing?" Asks Cunna.

Louis replies, "A threefold cord is not easily broken. One person praying is as a single strand …"

"…Then let us not keep my brother waiting, for perhaps our strands put together will help him to climb completely out of darkness to fully embrace our Great One's light …"

"…You're right. Steel has been prayed into sanctification and justified by entering into salvation's light out of the darkness. Now, we three shall combine our prayers so that he'll be released from his purge while going through all friction, heat, and fire 'til he fully enters the doorway of our Lord's peace and up before His throne of eternal light."

Out on the field before Calington Castle, Pine suddenly overcomes the prince. He lets his complaints be made known to the men while holding onto Edward after taking him by surprise. He cries out, "Something is going on with our leader and you'll have to trust me if you want to hold to our old ways."

Gray steps out from among the men and makes a stand, "We are under Cunna's word, which I for one will not break. You presume much, Pine. For it now appears as though you have a thirst for power that is interfering with your judgment." The men stand around observing what is taking place and hold their ground while being reminded of who's in charge.

Prince Edward then says, "Pine, your argument is not with me, but with the Creator of heaven and earth, for He is The Great One Himself. And as His wisdom says, 'Forgive them Father for they know not what they do,' release me now and there shall be no consequence on my part. Though if you continue to hold me, even though He is slow to anger, there might be some retaliation on His part. I suggest that you do not earn his wrath.'"

Pine realizes he is out numbered and quickly proclaims, "We are in a new land with new customs. Perhaps I should learn of them to prevent me from making other impulsive choices in the future. I am going to release you, Prince Edward, at thy word of no consequence. After all, I should at least learn of your ways. So that I may compare them to our own to see which way is better." Pine then releases Prince Edward and makes apology, "I am sorry for my behavior. I do not want you to believe we are without honor." Although, it is unbeknownst to everyone that his fingers are crossed behind his back.

Knocking is heard at the door to the rectory as they finish prayer.

The knocking continues and after their disappointment of not being able to fully release Steel from the dark realm, Andre opens the door. Cunna then suggests, "Perhaps Prince Edward has returned from the field to pray with us to release my brother with another cord of prayer." He then turns his head to discover King Liam.

He stands just inside the door and says, "I will tell my brother when I see him."

"King Liam! You are most welcome here."

"A light shone from on high. I was told by your prayers that I was to come and free Steel from out of the dark."

"Then you remember what I told you when I first arrived about my brother's predicament, which still moves me. For he lives within my mind and heart and tells me of his plight."

"I am here to help."

"You have my consent."

"I have forgiven you for the murder of my father, Steel. Yet there is something that hides beyond your thoughts within the dark. The fact that you've killed innocent blood still taunts you and you cannot forgive yourself for it."

Cunna answers what his brother impresses on his mind, *"It was the look upon his face. It was as though he anticipated what I was going to do and he let me cut off his head willingly. He smiled while at peace and this I cannot forget."*

"If it will help you to rest any easier, we all have slain The Lion-lamb of sacrifice. For it was for this purpose that The Great One came to earth and it was His joy set before Him to fulfill it. When I acknowledged it was for this purpose He was born, I understood what he meant by "Forgive them father for they know not what they do." And I can assure you that this was inside my father's heart, too. He chose the way that he did, just for you."

Cunna weeps with his brother, saying, "I have killed innocent blood as well. Though now, I receive peace in place of war. His blood that lives and floods the earth has redemptive power. A blood that I did not have or earn by my own merits. He laid down His life so I could be with Him and now I understand that I too, have slain this Lion-lamb. It was to appease my pain and I took pleasure in it. For by His splotches of red, I have crushed the serpents head and stepping over him, I have entered back into paradise as well. Now, my brother thanks you, too."

"Then let us send him off proper as anyone whose sins are forgiven are forgiven." King Liam steps forward and lays his hand upon Cunna's head and he goes down in the Spirit of blissful peace to the words, "I forgive and release you of your sins. Though they were as red as scarlet, now they are white as wool. Now, in the name of Jesus, they are retained no more."

Lying on the floor, Cunna has the appearance of being dead, but he is really at rest in a blissful peace. Until finally, upon opening his eyes, with a smile on his face, he speaks of how his brother has gone up and joined The Great One's light in a heavenly place.

A knock on the door is heard in the atmosphere of the room and Louis opens to Prince Edward. Once inside, he notices his brother Liam is there and inquires, "Did I miss something, Liam?"

The king motions with his head for him to have a look at Cunna and on seeing his inward smile, he nods with the words, "I guess I did."

Building of A New Kingdom

A meeting is taking place at court between King Liam and his brother, Edward. They are strategizing on how a new province of warriors could possibly come to fruition as a part of the Kingdom of Calington.

Prince Edward advises his brother, "Do you still feel it is a good idea to put Pine in charge as well as be the magistrate of law? Shouldn't there be some kind of checks and balances to maintain order? Haven't we already learned that absolute power corrupts?"

"On the other hand, could it not teach responsibility? Do not worry. Pine will discover that when he gets what he wants, he shall see the futility of it all, then desire something more. The men will keep

Pine in place. He will hear them or nothing will get accomplished."

"So, why not have a voice for the men to speak out if any injustice should happen? Won't it be better if they have someone to represent their voice?"

"I have observed that the voice of Gray has their ear already, we could appoint him and have favor with these men as well …"

"…And a second man could be voted on to hold a similar position, too. Then in case anything should happen to Gray, they would not be without a voice. They could consult each other, too. For there is always safety in the multitude of counsel."

"I see that referring to the notes in your journal while battling with spirits has made you very wise. Perhaps we shall use it to see how the words from the *Book of Life* shall be remembered in applying its knowledge to our life. In this way, we can properly divide the word of truth, lest we forget and lose the path of light within the darkness that dims a mind with pride before it blinds with night."

Prince Edward cmes to a conclusion, "After getting to know Pine and Cunna, I feel more suited to work with Pine and the others as we have already established a relationship."

"Having reported to me about Gray and Pine, I feel you bear much light on this matter. Good idea as I am acquainted with Cunna as well, though we must not forget that there is always an evil which lurks in the dark."

"Well, King Liam, I guess it takes a king to make a leader a king."

Liam turns to his brother and proclaims, "The pride of man could never achieve the righteousness of God as without faith all fall prey to the dark. For faith is not about denial, but the Spirit of truth which prevents all men from being lost."

"What is to be done?"

"I will train Cunna in our ways while you aid the others by helping them to build their kingdom as directed by The Great One's Spirit."

"I'm glad of the way all unfolds before us, my king."

Liam rises from his throne and bids his brother to come forward. Then after looking on each other for a moment, they embrace with a hug.

Prince Edward walks out on the field before the castle and encounters Pine as he reaches his tent. He watches the prince approach and lets out an apprehensive sigh before speaking, "What brings the good Prince Edward here today?"

"I have come to make good on my promise of putting the men to work. Would you care to discuss how this shall come to pass?"

"A prince that keeps his word, you do have my interest. Speak that I may know thee further.."

"Mark my words. From what I remember of my last visit here, I believe the men need a single voice as a chain of command, for it would save time in getting things done as you as magistrate must be in approval of a voice other than your own."

"Do you have an appointee in mind or are we to hold an election?"

"Both as it was considered that there is safety in the multitude of counsel …"

"…Who would that appointee be?"

"Well, Gray seems to have a voice that is in line with your leader and when he speaks all the men listen."

"Are you accusing me of being disloyal to Cunna?"

"Why would you say something like that?"

"I am entitled to my suspicions. Now, what comes after the men from our tribe know to honor the voice that speaks for them?"

"We shall break camp and start out for Nortica's Northwood Country where with the help of our carpenters, after the men use their brawn to fell trees and make a clearing, your own community gets built."

"Just like that, huh."

"Yeah! Just like that."

"You are a prince who keeps his word."

"Now, let's have that election which will determine who else shall have the peoples voice."

Pine speaks up, "Why not me?"

"Because this is to make your job easier. For when the men's voices are heard through a single voice, more can get decided quickly as you would only have to make decisions instead of get lost in endless arguments."

"Now that I fully understand this idea, we shall have that election."

At the castle, King Liam knocks on the door to Cunna's room. The door opens and the leader of the warrior says with a surprised look, "How is it that the king comes to me?"

"Do not look at my position, but rather as one man coming to speak with another."

Cunna steps back from the door and invites in King Liam, "I am eager to learn of the fresh perspective of your way. Enlighten my ears, what have you to say after experiencing The Great One for yourself, how has your perception changed?"

There is a pondering pause and then he speaks, "My roots of heritage have been supplanted as now I see with sight instead of just guessing my way through life. There is no more fear of the unknown but now there is a certainty that holds my heart which makes me grateful to face an eternity as I am alive. For once I was dead beneath lies that sparked all my hatred from being rotted within. I know this because after fighting against a darkness that I could not see to defeat in a fight, I was kept buried and restrained from knowing love inside my life."

"Beautifully said! As I can assure you, I am joined to your sentiment. Now that I am sure, we are seeing eye to eye in a like mindedness, we can discuss many things as there shall be a peace between us which will deepen our unity."

"Ruling to maintain peace and not instill fear to keep order, this doth sound refreshing. What is it you want to discuss that I may taste more of your words as they are like food for my soul …"

"…As your words are for mine. For it is known that we are friends by not only this, but a bond of love that sharpens to walk a path of even greater light as the diamond of truth is without price. So let us pray that no stray thoughts of spirit will try to have their way between us."

"Agreed."

"Join your hands with mine in peace so that our love may arise to join with the warmth of God's that we may send Him forth in our struggles 'til there be no more war."

After hands are joined, Liam instructs, "I want you to pray for us, Cunna. For you must get acquainted with your tongue being loosened while in conversation with our Maker."

"I understand." There is a pause and the leader of the warriors begins, "Lord, I am as a child before You. Guide me in what my requests must be, that our conversation shall be without strife. Amen!"

"Very well done. Now for our first order of business, an area of land has been picked out as a province for you and your men. How would you like it laid out?"

"You are giving us land?"

"You need a place to live, do you not?"

"There is no way that I could repay you, King Liam."

"I believe that the land I have in mind shall offer a solution as it is thick with trees, an arrangement can be made."

Cunna has a curious look and asks, "What would that be?"

"Our carpenters have been complaining about having to fell trees for lumber as it cuts in on their building time…"

"…Ahhh! You want us to share our lumber when clearing out trees from our province?"

"What will you call it?"

"I shall name it after my father. I will call it, Eridu."

"That is an excellent idea! Let us draw out the plans together, my friend. Perhaps while we work on them in the bond of The Great One's love, He will have something planned for us in the way of increasing our wisdom as we continue growing together."

Out on the trail, Prince Edward is on his horse riding next to Pine. Just behind them are wagons being drawn by horse. They carry forty men loaded with supply, carpenters, and tools.

Pine turns to Prince Edward and asks, "We have been traveling for quite awhile. How much further is it to our New Land of Eridu?"

"We'll be there before nightfall and have enough time to set camp if that what is troubling you."

"Speaking about things that trouble, I feel as though Cunna should be with us."

"He will be."

Prince Edward's accompaniment brightens up and cheerfully responds, "Then he'll soon join us?" '

"In the Spirit as He'll be praying."

"Why not now?"

"Because while the tribe is building a village, your leader shall be built into a kingdom where he'll not only be able to govern himself but the village you will build. For he shall have the wisdom of a king to rule it."

"Well, what about the election you spoke about for a second voice of the people?"

"Gray shall be an overseer of the crew and watch after them while I instruct the men according to the plans that Cunna had made …"

"…What doth that have to do with an election?"

"Gray will pick out the best two workers after a month and have the rest of the men vote between them."

The plans, the selection of vote, these ideas should have been run by me so I could decide if it was inline with our traditions."

"This expedition is being funded by an agreement between King Liam and your leader and as no coin from your tribe be involved, there is nothing to rule over."

"Then what am I supposed to do while all the work is being done?"

"All hands will be needed for the work that is set before us until it is finished."

"Doth that mean you, too?"

"Yes."

"Why have we stopped?"

Prince Edward motions with his head.

Pine responds after seeing a wall of trees, "There has gotta be a better place. The trees are too thick here."

"This is the spot, magistrate." Turning his head, he gives direction, "Gray, instruct the men to make camp."

"Yes, majesty."

Back at the castle Suzy is excited about the return of her mother, Queen Ashley. Though, all is not what it seems to be as her uncle, the Monsignor at the monastery has died. In addition, her grief over King Henry's death has opened the wound of the passing of her uncle again. So, instead of embracing her daughter she remains distant and unintentionally passes her by with teary eyes.

Suzy cries out, "Mom, are you okay?"

"I can't talk now dear," is her response and she continues on her way.

The next few days, Ashley sets things in order until things settle down. She has overlooked spending time with Suzy and now she is nowhere to be found. She goes to her husband, now King Liam, and inquires of him where to find Suzy. He responds, "She looked rather bored, so I suggested she go with my brother to see the building of the province of Eridu, for a change in pace."

"Was that the band of men I saw leaving on the wagons when arriving at the castle the other day?"

"Quite right."

"They looked to be such a rough lot of men and she is without full presence of mind. Do you really believe she'll be all right?"

"Edward knows to keep an eye on her, the trip will do her good. Besides, she'll get to see the transformation of the men which should encourage her faith."

"It is true that her faith wavers, perhaps you're right."

"A fresh adventure like this should take the impetuousness of her youth out of her."

The queen takes the king's hand and says, "What you say makes sense."

It Happened in Eridu

Axes in hands chop away at the trunks of many trees. Pine sees fair Princess Suzy walking with her uncle. Edward suggests to her, "Stay back from the wagon while I help the men." The magistrate then has ideas on how he can preserve the traditions of the elders.

He goes to the wagon where they are loading logs and has a plan fully conjured up in his mind to take Calington castle for himself. Looking around, he sees an opportunity to put it into action. He manages to grasp the rope being used to tie down some logs for transport. Next, when no one is watching, he cuts half way into it before stepping away. He next makes his way over and positions himself near Suzy.

There are two men on top of the pile of heavy logs being set as toppers in their position. All at once the rope cut that held the lower logs in place snaps near the rear and the man at the back of the wagon falls beneath some of the logs and gets crushed. Prince Edward and the others rush to aid him while Princess Suzy becomes nauseous at the sight of all the blood. Pine walks over and says, "You don't look so well, princess, perhaps you better step away. Let me get you out of the sun as well as my tent is nearby."

"Thank you, magistrate."

He helps her to walk while overcoming her nausea and they enter his tent. "After seeing what you just saw, you need something to steady you." He adds a little white powder to a vessel filled with water from a scoop in his hand out of a large jar and gives it to Princess Suzy. "Here drink this down."

"What is it?"

"It is something that will make you feel much better. I shall join you as I do not have a stomach for blood anymore. It makes me queasy."

The two raise their glasses and toast, but when pine goes to drink he only touches it to his lips and pretends to drink as Suzy drinks her's down. "Oh, you're right, Pine. It doth make me feel wonderful. Can I have some more?"

"Of course, my princess, only if I give you more you must not tell anyone else."

"Why not?"

"Do you want more?"

"Yes."

"Then heed my word."

"Alright, I will."

"Here, let me fill your water skin and when you run out, you can always come back for more. Perhaps if you keep returning with your uncle, I'll be able to keep accommodating you."

She looks out the tent before leaving and turning back, she says, "I'll return on the morrow."

The sun has its way as it shines, breaking through the clouds. It is taken as a sign for everyone looking on. Prince Edward looks over to his niece, but she refuses to acknowledge his nod and motion for her to come over. He then regains his focus while Princess Suzy keeps to herself. The rays of light continue to shine down on the fallen warriors open grave before all.

The Prince proclaims, "The Great One acknowledges our fellow warrior with His light this day. Although Trung has died during this time of peace, he fought like a warrior at his work to preserve his heritage with his silent voice. I have presence of mind that he is no different than anyone else here. His intentions were honorable in the simplicity of his life and it is only fitting that he be buried at the entrance of the land of Eridu, a place of rest that he can call a home of his own.

Gray becomes involved, "As my voice is for the many among us, I move that the road leading into our province be called, 'Trung Road.'"

The voice of the magistrate cries out while approaching, "That road was supposed to be named after me. I forbid it!"

Prince Edward intervenes, "Grey holds the voice of the people, which are many. Your voice stands alone, Pine. For as Trung died on a road that was cleared by Calington labor originally, the sign post will be mounted on our property as well. So, you are overruled. The road leading into Eridu will remain Trung."

"Very well. You had your say. Now, I will have mine. Because Cunna appointed me the first magistrate, I should at least have the road that passes before the courthouse named Pine."

"Sounds reasonable to me," says Gray.

"Good! Then it is settled."

Prince Edward then asks, "What is that you carry?"

Pine answers, "As we are at a time of peace and not war, I thought it only fitting that a wooden training sword be buried with him."

Gray nods his head and says, "As voice of the people, that is something I am sure everyone would agree upon."

Prince Edward is nodding in agreement when his niece catches his eye. He then calls to her, "Suzy, you don't look to good. Have you taken ill?"

"Today has been very draining, uncle."

"I know what you saw was a lot this day, even for myself as a grown man it was a bit much. We shall spend the night here rather than return to the castle as I'll not have you fainting on the way."

Pine offers, "Perhaps you two would like to share my tent tonight?"

The crickets chirp loudly in the moonlight alongside the road, signifying a hot day on the morrow. Prince Edward steps outside the tent and walks a few paces to relieve himself. The noise from its flap folding back awakens Pine who notices the princess shivering in the warmth of night. He whispers softly to her, "Shhh! Drink some more of your special water."

"I finished it!"

"That was supposed to last 'til you came back tomorrow."

She begins to shake as she answers, "I didn't know."

His jar is quickly opened and some powder scooped up into the palm of the magistrates hand. Going to her side, he says, "Breathe this in your nose and you'll be okay for now, but come see me on the morrow at noon and I will instruct you on what next to do."

After inhaling the powder, her shaking stops and both settle down. Moments later, Prince Edward returns and settles in as well.

The sun rises as footsteps walk the ground. A few moments later, Prince Edward and his niece are discovered to meet Gray by the supply wagon.

"Ahhh! Gray. So, voice of the people. Are you ready to go over the plans on how the Eridu province will look when it is finished?"

"Yes and afterwards, we'll lunch."

Princess Suzy notices that her shadow is almost gone and starts to become fidgety while Edward climbs into the supply wagon and looks for the plans. "Now where did those plans get to? Ah! Yes, here they are." When the prince looks back towards Gray, he notices that Suzy has gone but shrugs it off, saying, "I guess she got hungry when you mentioned lunch. No matter, we'll catch up with her later."

Princess Suzy looks around and upon seeing no one, she quickly enters Pine's tent.

Looking over he says to her, "You have come just in time for my spell to take away your cravings, dirt."

"What do you mean by that?"

"It means you belong to me by the use of my drug and the way to end its ownership over you is to be complete with me. For by closing a circle in union with me, you will break the spell of the drug…Now look. See this pill I hold?"

"I see it."

"You are to fish it out of my mouth with your tongue, during a dance we shall have and swallow it. She steps forward and tries to start dancing with him.

"Ahhh! Not so fast as there is something you must do for me first. I even believe you will find it more enjoyable than what you've already experienced, dirt."

"I don't like being called that!"

"Then sit, my flower, and lay on the ground within the spelling circle I have drawn. For you shall open your petals unto me quickly that I may plant my seed in your garden. Or, you will always contain the filth of the drug which makes you dirt. A painful existence you will bear while in its grasp forever."

The shock of Pine's words overwhelm her as he continues, "You are of age, bear me a child! Then in four years hence, you shall return with my brat, which shall learn of the ways of our old country. Now, you are never to let anyone know what has happened here, nor that I am the father or you both shall die.

Going down on the ground, Princess Suzy starts to cry silently and as her tears begin to flow. Pine stands before her smiling.

"Silent tears become you. Let us keep it this way during and after our dance." He then places the pill in his mouth while taking a step forward.

Back in The Present

Almost five years have passed since the incident at Eridu. Suzy has bore a son and managed to hold to Pine's request of keeping things quiet. This has locked her within the secrecy of her own soul. After living in fear most of the time, she has now become weary in keeping illusive to honor the pact between Pine and herself. The sound of her fears from the silence of her mind becomes deafening while she waits for the proper timing to arrive.

Princes Ronan's bond with his grandfather grows strong as time passes by. It allows him to forget his daughters shame and mysterious silence which happened on her return from Eridu. It was suspected that having her son out of covenant with God was the cause, but her mother Ashley suspected more. King Henry even advised Suzy to seek counsel with the healer or the priests, suggesting they could help her. Yet, she has chosen to remain locked away inside herself without even a peep while paying him no mind. A few times she has tried to find solace in the woods, but even here Pine mysteriously came upon her to increase the tension of her fears to keep her blinded of all else except their pact.

A few days after Prince Ronan and Princess Suzy had gone missing, Sargent James reports back to King Liam with full report, "Your Majesty, it took me quite some time, but I know where your daughter and grandson are."

"Well, where did you track them?"

"I had the fortune of dry weather with low wind the past few days, so I was able to find their trail on the open road after a lot of back tracking outside the castle grounds. Discovering the foot prints of a small boy with that of a young woman leaving the area, I could tell it was your grandson and daughter's prints by matching up their extra pair of shoes on the ground."

"Where did their trail end?"

" Eridu!"

"Curious, why would she go there of all places? Unless Ronan's father dwells there in hiding all the while. Did you happen to enter Eridu and see what doorway their prints led?"

"There were too many prints on the ground. Even with some triple back tracking, it still remains unknown where they disappeared amongst the many steps before the courthouse on the street of Pine."

"Thank you, Sergeant James. I am sure my brother is not too far. So, if you should see him on the way out please have him come in."

Prince Edward enters the door with words on his tongue, "You know me too well, my King."

Sargent James says while passing him by, "I knew you were there, too." He then leaves the king to face his brother. "Another time you show your face after my disappointment. It was more tolerable for her to come home pregnant under your very watch then for my grandson to be taken from me. For there is an evil at work here, which I sense even now attempts to destroy me. If it were not for the fact that I knew he was prepared, having met our Lord before he was taken it might have done me in. Although, God being one step ahead of evil my hope lays within the fact that one day I will see him again in the light of heaven if not here."

"You spoke well, my brother, and I am sorry for the silence that you will once again endure."

"Discovering my daughter's silence when she was with child and out of covenant with the Lord was hard enough, and now the silence of the absence of my grandson. I trusted you to look out for Princess Suzy on her trip to Eridu. Holding my peace when you brought her back spoiled had left a darkness within my soul that I again am reminded of by this second loss. It doth not make it any less painful even though I know somehow this must be a part of God's plan, too. Oh, the evil of this! For I know that in addition to missing Ronan, he is the one who will suffer more as learning how to love has become a root of suffering for him."

Prince Edward speaks in a counseling tone of voice, "I pray that The Great One shall continue to have His way. I besiege thee to stay focused on how

He will bless us all throughout this ordeal. For if you continue to allow yourself to get upset any further, evil will not only drain the substance of your life but become stronger, Liam."

"We all have limitations which need to be exceeded or how else shall we grow? Yet we must overcome them without losing any balance from having peace or we shall return to the mouth of darkness, which awaits to feed on us once again."

"I hear father's wisdom speaking through you, my brother. Now let me add to it. You shall go to Eridu and enquire of Cunna about my daughter and grandson and see if he knows anything of their whereabouts as he has become a strong ally and can be trusted."

"What if he doth not know where they are?"

"Then you will enquire of Gray as he is the voice of the people."

"What if she is in hiding?"

"I shall send Sergeant James and another guard. They shall carry coin for anyone who can locate them during your excursion. If need be, have decree posters which offer reward made. Post them if they cannot be found after three days. Someone has had to have seen something."

"I will do as you have requested of me." But as he starts on his way, Liam calls to him, "Edward."

After turning back to face his brother, they make eye contact and the king continues to speak while nodding his head, "Thank you!"

From the jail beneath the courthouse at Eridu, a very faint voice cries out from a solitary cell. It has no windows and all is dark. After not being heard for quite a while, Ronan curls up in a corner and begins to sob.

He here's a voice from the other side of the door which mocks him, "Oh! Boo, hoo, hoo. If you quit your bawling, you unwanted brat and promise to behave, I will look after you," is the voice of Pine, speaking to him in a loud and frightening manner.

"That's not true," Ronan weeps in response.

"You're only here because your grandfather doth not want you anymore."

"Liar!"

"Oh! Am I? Why do you believe you're here?"

"I don't know."

"That is why you are in a dark place right now. For here in the darkness is a truth that every man can understand. For a mind that is dark can make its own light and create a life to choose whatever it wants to be in life."

"One day you shall stand before the truth of light!"

"The truth is, you are in a dark place and I am not."

"I am not afraid of your dark light!"

"You put up a bold front, but you are afraid because you choose to be so."

"You do not know if I am afraid or not!"

"I have powers that you know nothing of. Yet, if you choose to be a warrior then you'll never be afraid again, brat!

"I do not like being called that!"

"Then be a warrior and ignore my words, for then you'll find peace within the dark. For once at rest while facing the unknown, you can conquer it."

Pine opens a slot towards the bottom of the door before a lit candle and drops in the knife that was given him by the priest from his old country. The light from the candle shines through the opening. "Pick up the knife and get a firm grip on its handle."

"What for?"

"A warrior can only protect himself from what is unknown in the dark with a weapon, brat!"

"How do you know I will not use it on you?"

"Spoken like a true warrior already, brat! However, a good question deserves a good answer. You will not kill me for two reasons. One is because what I am teaching intrigues you …" A latch is heard and the door opens revealing Pine standing before him in the candlelight and holding a cat that he pets…"And two, I am your father."

A "Clang!" is heard as the blade of his knife hits the floor from Ronan's open hand as a "Noooooo!" of an out cry is heard.

Ronan backs away into the corner and once again curls up to comfort himself as pine lowers the cat, "Here I brought you some company, brat!" Pine lowers the cat which goes right to his son and rubs itself up against him as it starts to purrr! "…And it is your exit out of this chamber. For unless you kill this cat, you shall not leave this place alive."

"The Great One shall deliver me!"

"How can you trust in the memory of a king who rejected you? And as for The Great One, you may be set free in your spirit, but your body shall surely die locked away in darkness and forgotten …Your spirit without a body will not do you much good. Will it, brat!"

"Never will I kill this cat."

"Then, I guess you do not want to live. For when it gets hungry enough, after you pass out from your lack of resources it will eat you."

Pine closes the door to the cell leaving his son in the dark once again. A few moments later the slot opens in the door and he says, "If you do not want to do it for yourself, do it for me and I will get the blame. Oh, did I mention that the cat is very hungry. I, for one, want you to live, but you can choose to die."

Tears fill Ronan's eyes as the slot closes in the door leaving him in the dark yet another time.

"Kill it and you shall overcome your fears and become a warrior forever. Find your knife and do it now."

"I do not Know how," is heard from inside the cell.

Pine instructs from outside the door, "Put the knife under its throat and pull strait down towards its tail and it will be over before you know."

"I cannot do it!"

"No food or water until you do!"

"It is not within me!" Ronan sobs from the other side of the door."

"He next observes the cat's eyes glowing in the dark."

"I cannot believe you're going to choose to die like a sniveling coward!" Fear grips Ronan's eyes.

"I'm, sorry!" Is heard before a cat call outside the door.

Pine opens the door to young, Ronan. He stands while staring covered in blood with the knife in his hand. His father collects the knife and lifts his son into arms and says while patting his head, "Good lad! You belong to me now."

Ronan responds by throwing up and Pine begins to laugh, "Ha! Good, lad!" He then takes his son and locking him in a large open cell with food and water says, "It be best you be kept out of sight for now. I'll be back on the morrow with a change of clothes as you must get acquainted with what it is to be on the battlefield for now. Then when you're older, you shall defeat all of those who have abandoned you."

Pine's son goes over and sits on the floor beneath a window while beginning to eat his evening meal covered in blood and puke. "Clang!" The sound of the knife hits the jail cell floor as his father says, "Your're going to need this, warrior." The boy continues to eat impervious to all else. The footsteps of pine can be heard walking away.

Soon after, the sun starts to set while he chews with a blank stare in his eyes. He eats only to feed his hunger and nothing more.

Horse hooves fall in the streets of Eridu's province and three riders enter its town. Prince Edward instructs the sergeant, "James, go to the general store and see if any purchases of children's clothes have been made as of late while me and Private York find Cunna at his villa to see if he has heard anything about Ronan. We'll meet back here on Pine Street before the court house at twelve o'clock sun."

"Yes, Majesty!"

Splitting up, they start on their separate ways.

A bucket of water is poured over Pine's son in a bath by his mother. Pine then hands him a towel that he takes and drys himself off with. The princess then opens a burlap sack with a change of clothes for her boy and while handing them over says, "Put these on."

Pine instructs Suzy as he hands her the soiled clothes, "Get these cleaned up!"

"Why are you so rough?"

While smiling, he says, "It's good for the boy to know how to treat a lady." Turning his back on the boy's mother, he notices that his son is already dressed. Suzy leaves while Pine orders the boy to step over to the window. "Come here, lad." The boy walks over to his father who lifts him up and looking through the bars, the magistrate tells him, "See all this? One day it shall be yours and so much more. For I run this town and everyone in it is subject to my rule, brat!"

The sun shines down from above the courthouse and casts no shadows for it is noon. Sergeant James looks over after tying his horse on a hitching post. While in front of the horse, he sees Prince Edward approaching with the private who bears the purse with coin. "Did you find anything out, sergeant?" asks the prince.

"It seems we've come to the right place," says James.

"How so?"

"It seems that Pine picked up some children's clothes for a small boy early this morn."

"I'm glad that you found out more than I. For Cunna knew nothing and I could not find Gray."

A small bell chimes on the back of the door upon entering the courthouse. After a few moments, Pine appears in an official looking open robe at its front. It symbolizes his official position as magistrate. He takes a seat behind a large desk and looking up notices Prince Edward who is standing before him. He asks, "What brings your majesty to our province this day?"

"I come to make inquiry of Princess Suzy and her son, Prince Ronan."

"What leads you to believe that they reside in Eridu?"

"They were tracked and their trail ends here."

"The mother seeks sanctuary in a place where King Liam has no rule and our customs holds for her boy as well."

"Those who fear the truth have eyes painted with lies and rot inside themselves."

"Gibberish to me!"

"I would like to speak to them and make sure that they are okay."

"They are in capable hands."

"I would like to speak to the boy's father."

"He wishes to remain anonymous and as he is the owner of his property he has informed me that they are not to be questioned."

"I must press this issue on behalf of his grand-father, King Henry."

"In accordance with your laws, you have no say how we are to rule in our province unless you want to disrupt the balance of rule throughout all of Calington. However, I am not unreasonable. So, I will permit the king a chance to present his case with the use of one of our lawyers who is familiar in our common practices. A fee will be necessary to cover our necessary court costs of course."

"Are you trying to extort us?"

"Since you are unaware of our practices, I will let your remark go unpunished. Any further outbursts will cost you a fine. Do I make myself clear?"

"Yes, your honor."

Pine brings down a gavel on the desk, "You are free to go."

On the street outside the courthouse, Sergeant James makes comment upon seeing the prince, "You look like you have seen a ghost."

"Probably would have been better off if I had."

"What happened in there?"

"The Magistrate is corrupt with a darkened mind and I see that justice will be hard to find here."

"What of the king's daughter and grandson?"

"They are safe, but we have no jurisdiction in this province to have them released."

Private York speaks up before the other two, "We have The Great One!"

James looks to the prince, "We do at that!"

Prince Edward comments to the other two, "We have a message to deliver to King Henry, then we shall see what our Lord will do."

The three mount their horses and start on their way.

The Magistrate enters a door and within the darkness he starts to converse with an old familiar voice, it is that of the Dark One which begins to speak, "Vengeance on King Liam through Suzy's actions has already begun to take place. Though be advised, do not let Ronan get close to any who speak truth or we may have problems."

"Most men here are dim of wit, you need not worry."

"Have you not heard that Cunna, your king, had returned a few days ago?"

"I wonder why I was not informed?"

"A king doth not have to inform anybody of anything! Are you as dim as you say the others are in this province, too?"

"Are you saying that he is spying out how things are being run?"

"I'm saying that he might break the warriors spell that I've instructed you to place upon the brat! If his bond of truth were rekindled within him, a flash of light could strengthen his mind and interfere with all."

"Need I remind that after this trial, once the mother of the brat's life is taken by him, he'll be shocked out of existence."

"My serpent tongue on your breath still serves me well. You shall paint the picture of her betrayal of promise of having power for anything she desires on his mind exquisitely, I'm sure. When the brat is manipulated into being shocked by believing our unrecognized deception of lies of his mother's desires, the release of such a darkness shall strengthen me with a freedom to make every mind in Eridu black. Between her hatred over her despised love for you, my magistrate, and how she has hurt her son, this alone has increased my darkness already."

"I understand now that when the brat murders his mother his fate will be sealed."

"You shall bring me a joy which will darken even more than my heart as hatred in place of love is such a powerful tool in the bringing down of kingdoms."

"Do not forget that I am the vehicle behind all of your deception!"

"Do not worry, Calington will cave by way of my intrusion. It shall be yours. Then the darkness of your heritage will be preserved as you've requested. You shall gain favor by using the brat at Calington Court and as evil will do good in serving both of our purposes well, you need not worry. For what lurks in darkness will always prevail in this world to serve everyone well."

"You have trained me for the purpose of using good to serve evil by deceit. I know it will pay off as no one wants to sacrifice for the truth anymore.

There is such a powerful grip when there's a lipser-vice that keeps hearts cold towards The Great One's warmth from sparking love."

"You must make sure that there are no more slips. For when Queen Shirley was reunited with Norris of Nortica, a light went forth with love that nearly did me in."

"There is always a darkness that produces strife and very shortly at the trial, it shall suck away King Liam's life where maintaining your cloak of power here on earth will continue to defeat anything that's not truly bright."

The Trial

$\mathbf{B}$ack at the castle, a meeting is taking place between King Liam, Queen Ashley, Prince Edward, and the healer.

Prince Edward shares what is upon his heart after presenting the facts of his meeting with The Magistrate, "So, could we not somehow bend our laws without breaking them by appealing to the people through Gray? Surely, once they know what Pine is doing, he will be made to feel pretty unpopular after learning of the plight of your situation. Afterall, did you not forgive the death of your father and help them to establish Eridu in the first place?"

"No, they would exalt him. For looking after them in facing it off with a king in their interests would strengthen the darkness of their old customs even more, which we don't want. My brother, you must remember that the Kingdom of truth has an established base to build upon. It cannot be altered or evil would cleave into it with a practiced lie. You must know by now that our inner struggles for peace could not be solved without a firm foundation of truth built upon Christ, for He is stability itself. At one time you had an inner turmoil that existed, too. Did you forget? Is this not true?"

Prince Edward bows his head and speaks with a sobermind, "Thank you for this reminder, my king, as darkness once again had crept in."

The healer becomes involved, "Doth not your majesty forget that Cunna has become a very strong ally? Could he not command the release of your grandson immediately?"

"He has his own position to consider in this matter. For if he were to reverse a tribal custom to suit the purposes of another country from the outside, it would create a faction in his own leadership. One that the magistrate, whom he has appointed, could rise up in opposition and presume leadership over.

For once the truth of an internal custom is broken, everything can become shaken loose.

You have been silent, Ashley. Is there anything that you would like to contribute in the way of an idea?"

Looking over from her seat, she lets her heart be known, "How soon you all forget that we have customs, too. We have the right of public record of each affair concerning the royal family in the line of succession of heritage. I'm sure that pine would find it objectionable if the case were documented for Ronan to read at a later time. As once light was brought to this situation, the voice of true reason would spark light towards a just rule later on. This is our hope as truth speaks louder and brings light to expel the darkness of any lie to those who would receive it. The Great One shall always rule as His is the voice of reason even though we shall be defeated at court miserably. The truth of the matter will live on as an act of love, lain down, that Ronan will one day grow to understand for the sake of a soundness of mind that will effect an entire future generation which will surround him. As once the head is in its proper place, the rest of the body follows."

"I see that the love of truth shall once again prevail in the end. Thank you, my queen."

A variety of tents start to appear on the main road outside the province of Eridu as messages that were sent for character witnesses have been received and many have come. Soon, word gets back to the Magistrate and seeking guidance from his dark friend, he enters their room and quietly closes the door 'til all is dark.

"Back for more advice I see!" says the dark hooded figure in the room."

"There's enough people on the road now to easily overthrow us."

"Do not be alarmed as King Liam is a man of honor …"

"But, I have taken his grandson!"

"The king shall uphold his word as all men of honor do. You can rely on this. So, relax!"

"I will be glad when all of this is all over."

"The brat's mind is almost ripe with enough darkness to do his mother in and then no one will know about you being his father. Just keep him out of sight and away from people who bear light and he shall remain in my darkness of night. Now, have you sent out the ten invites to your men to cover your tracks and keep things legal?"

"I must say that you have really set everything up perfectly."

"It's simple, I enjoy being evil …"

"…And if it gets me what I want, so do I!"

"In the morning on the morrow, King Liam arrives with the keeper of the royal records before the road leading into the province of Eridu. Everyone who shall bear witness mounts up on his behalf and forms a line behind the entourage of Prince Edward, Queen Ashley, and the healer which are followed by the royal guard. Kelth and Bumba ride up alongside the king as everyone else falls in line behind the guard to complete the procession. Edward whistles and the advance guards ride up Trung Road and station themselves before the courthouse on Pine.

When the magistrate hears about how his ten invited men were searched while entering the court, he rises and goes back to meet the Dark One in the room of night again. The voice of evil speaks from the darkness, "They are trying to intimidate you, but that is all which can be done. Trust me! Their dimness cannot outshine my darkness, for they have exhausted all their light. Now, go and watch their Spirit fail them as a setting sun at night. Take thy rightful place anew and see thy chapter be written this day in your lands to come as all will fade in memory when you are on the throne."

Upon returning to the court room, Pine notices that King Liam has already arrived with much company that surrounds him. Gray announces, "All rise for the honorable Magistrate." It becomes quiet as everyone stands.

Pine sits at the desk and taps it with a gavel, "The court is in session. You may be seated." Pine then notices that Cunna is sitting with King Liam and makes comment, "I see that you have chosen adequate council that is familiar with the common practice of our laws." He next looks to Gray. "Has the court fee been acquired, Gray?"

"Yes, it has."

"Then we will proceed."

"Cunna rises and makes first presentation, "The first character witness I call is Kelth, chief of the tribe of Nomads."

The Magistrate interrupts, "that will not be necessary. Your fine character is not what is in question here, but the law of our land and the custom of our edicts of tradition are what is being challenged."

Cunna turns to the keeper of the royal records and says, "Let it be noted that character witnesses to establish that seed of thought from another culture has been denied."

Public record is not permissible in this court as Eridu is a province unto itself outside of public lands. You know that you have no jurisdiction in our land?"

"Yes, I know." King Liam whispers something into Cunna's ear who responds, "The record in question is being taken for the concerns of only private matters of heritage of the royal family, which at their discretion can be made public and this is in line with both our laws and traditions."

"According to the laws and practices of our people, I rule in this court as the judge from the edicts of our old country. Know it now, King Liam. Cunna's words only cary weight here as they are within the precedents of our existing laws. However, our laws further state that the father, being from our country, owns the boy and has full possession of him as his property, regardless of what you would consider to be in the best interests of the boy."

Cunna states, "According to the ruling of our laws, the father must be present at the court in order to defend his property."

Pine calls to the warriors he has invited to the court and says, "Would you raise your hands with me please?" All raise an arm along with Pine who continues to speak, "One of these men who holds his hand in the air is the boy's father. More than ten hands that are raised on a matter and this signifies our whole tribe when put to a vote. The boy and his mother have now been established as property of our whole tribe."

Kelth stands, "I've had enough of this! I stand for my people in saying, you shall no longer receive grain or seed from us until Prince Ronan is released …And I am sure that there are others who feel the same way in this room!"

"I feel the same way you do," says Cunna.

King Liam agrees, "…As do I, but let us fulfill all righteousness as to not repay an evil with another evil that will cause a whole tribe to suffer."

"Then there is no need to punish the tribe. For me being the leader of Eridu will not permit this ruling as it is my right to do so," says Cunna.

Bumba speaks up as well, "Then this brings us back to the beginning."

Prince Edward interjects, "Can nothing be resolved?"

"The father is allowed to remain anonymous and the laws of our customs are now made known so that they shall be preserved. I would say that a lot is being accomplished here this day," says Pine.

Cunna confirms, "It is true that as long as the father is present as known by the office of The Magistrate, his identity doth not need to be revealed as to incriminate himself to any charges within the culture of our old country," says Cunna.

"This is permissible?" asks Prince Edward.

"Let your private records note this," says Gray.

Pine addresses everyone in the room, "You will rise for the court's decision." King Liam stands as the Magistrate continues, "This court has determined that your beliefs, being contrary to ownership of the mother and the child is deemed stressful on how the child shall be raised. Therefore in accordance with our laws and practices, which you as a reminder have granted in accordance with your laws that holds all of our lands together. You shall not be allowed any visitation with Ronan at all for as long as the father deems it fit should he so choose to remain in our province. The boy will remain the property of the father. King Liam as it is the wish of the father, you are not allowed back in our province until his property is transferred or released."

King Liam then states, "Then I will buy the boy and release him from his bond."

"The father has stated that he is not for sale at any price. You are now free to go and should you attempt to contact the boy, heavy fines will be imposed for breaking our laws.

King Liam looks to the royal keeper of records who says, "I have it all, your majesty."

The magistrate brings down the gavel, "Court closed!"

King Liam's head goes down with his chin touching his chest and he freezes for a few moments before sitting back down.

Cunna, leaning forward whispers into King Liam's ear, "The truth will live on when I encounter your grandson, So, just as you have taught, have faith!"

Liam enquires, "Cunna, what just happened here?"

"Order was just maintained so that The Great One will continue to have his way."

He slowly nods his head and says, "Thank you for your encouragement."

Pine rises and quickly goes to the dark room and reports to the Dark One in their meeting place. Everyone else slowly starts to file out of the room and it is noticed that in the midst of an outcome of misery the king still glows, he has not lost his faith.

King Liam and Cunna finally make it to the front door when the leader remembers, "If you want to tarry for a moment or two, King Liam, I have a matter protocol to tend as I must shake hands with Pine and congratulate him on his job well done. Even though I am not happy, I still have to live here with him."

"I quite understand. I will be outside, my friend," says the king.

The rays from a four o'clock sun hang low as they shine through the low barred windows to the jail cells in its basement.

Ronan returns to himself again from having a blank stare and realizes he is looking at his mother.

"Mother, why did you bring me back to father and to this bad place?"

"I was threatened by the Magistrate. He said that he would kill not only me, but you and grandfather if I did not bring you to him when you turned four."

"Why did you choose somebody like father to be with?"

"It was more like he chose me as I was raped."

"Outside of knowing my grandfather, I am sorry that I was ever born into this world."

"You have a knife. Why not use it on Pine when he least suspects and then we could be free of him."

"Because I realize that if I kill, I would become just like him and never be free of him."

Pine's voice suddenly disrupts their conversation.

"Just like all witches who sell their souls for power, your mother lies as she seduced me into her scheme to possess all of Calington through your birth. Why else would she leave the Castle to come live in a land of few comforts and break your grand-father's heart unless she had a pact with the devil himself."

During the intensity of their discussion, some approaching footsteps in the background go unnoticed.

"The boy's mind is young and fertile with impressions, I would rather have him use the knife on me than believe any of your lies as your tongue cuts like a lash upon what is left of my heart." Princess Suzy begins to sob.

Pine claps his hands and says, "What a performance, you almost had me believing you. It would be best if you silenced her manipulative tongue for the sake of everyone by taking her up on her offer. For the venom that is within her is worthy of death unlike the cat, warrior. Is love not worth more than money? Kill your enemy and we shall rule together. Kill her before she kills you as she is capable of anything!"

"Mother, how could you believe that money is worth more than love?"

"No! Ronan! No!"

The silent footsteps become revealed to be Cunna's voice as he speaks out as a beacon of light that sparks forth the reason of truth to the situation, "You do not have to listen to Pine, Ronan. For as heir to King Liam's throne, you not only rule over him, but as his son the province of Eridu as well."

"I am your father, brat! You are to listen as you are of my blood and belong to me!"

"Your name is Ronan and not brat! Take a stand now and reclaim your right to the throne as its heir. Now is the acceptable time for all to be set right!"

In a flash of brilliance, Ronan recognizes the voice of the light of truth from Cunna's mouth as the same wisdom of his grandfather by what has just been said. Cunna continues, "Remember, friendship with The Great One and be careful what you do, for it may set the course for the rest of your life."

Pine looks to him and says, "Kill her and you shall regain control of your life, my boy!"

"I am not your boy, for I have a friend that is greater than you and He says to forgive them Father for they know not what they do."

"Kill her and you shall receive your rightful heritage."

Ronan turns to Pine in anger at first and says, "Let not the sun go down on your wrath." He then throws his knife to the ground and further says, "I forgive you for not knowing that The Great One is a giver of life and not death. We only bring judgement upon ourselves when our actions turn wrong. I will not allow your darkness to rest on me any longer as it has been boken by words of light. Christ came to the earth to show us mercy through His life and restore all with His love of true light."

Pine suddenly cries out, "Meddler!" and charges towards Cunna. The Magistrate pushes the leader into the bars and he bangs his head against one of them and slides down to the floor. Pine goes to kick him, but when Cunna grabs his foot he wrestles him to the ground causing Pine to drop his keys which spill into Suzy and Ronan's cell. Suzy is quick to pick up the keys and unlock the barred door as they wrestle each other.

Cunna suddenly pushes pine forward and the princess quickly pushes the door open into Pine's head, knocking him out.

"Quick, come out of there!" When they do, Cunna drags Pine in and locks the door after all are out before removing the key.

Suzy looks to her son with tears in her eyes and says, "Ronan, I have had a hatred towards your grandfather and it has not only taught me to hate myself but every one around me. I only see this because of your words and actions which have now balanced out my soul. Your God has now created a light of life within me, too. We shall leave this province, return to the castle, and be reconciled to my father to receive our rightful heritage of love. I need to receive this in place of all the darkness of death I have been walking in."

Cunna says, "Much light has been spoken here this day. For you have discovered the true path of peace by honoring The Great one, which truly happens by not being obedient out of guilt but love."

Pine suddenly lets out a loud cry and begins to shake himself awake while on the floor in convulsions by what speaks through him in a demonic voice, "The castle is besieged by darkness while you've been away, for the queen's twin brother even now crosses the bridge from the parallel of worlds where Calington has already fallen by the dark choice of King Naha's greed. I will tell you all how Ashley's twin made a deal with this king if you let me remain from within my vessel of Pine's. It is me who rules by my disturbance inside of him. It's the only way you can enter into battle to defeat evil once and for all. For when it has no place to slip back and forth between worlds to do man harm, he shall be kept from being double mindedly two faced again."

Ronan becomes involved, "Do not speak with it, Cunna! Lest you be deceived into letting its darkness within your soul as well. For just as a double minded man is unstable in all his ways, a kingdom divided against itself cannot stand. So, do not believe its lies by communicating with what lives in him. For a warrior wars against the truth of life that death sparks a vengeance of what belongs to God's Spirit alone. This liar cannot divide itself against its own spirits of this world. Cleverly it still deceives to live and breathe by single darkened choice within the minds of men.

For I know that only God's Spirit is stronger by the Great One who is Christ while invited in daily. Or, the confusion of darkness would allow a crazy mind to rule again. I see this well as I've now been taught, for I have fully remembered my first love by the light and life of all men.

Now Cunna, you and I must pray while my mother goes to reconcile with her father as we with truth must protect the interior castle wall within his mind that has been weakened this day inside him."

Princess Suzy eagerly says, "I go!"

Cunna looks to Ronan and says, "From out of the mouth of babes!"

"…And the righteous who are as bold as lions, now let us pray."

All is Laid to Rest

King Liam is speaking to his brother in front of the courthouse, all at once he beholds his eyes looking at something from behind him. Then he turns his head to see Princess Suzy standing behind him with a look in her eyes as she says, "Why are you looking at me in such a surprised manner?"

"There is something different about your eyes."

"Then you can tell?"

"Welcome home!"

"I wanted to surprise you."

"It still is …and a pleasant one at that, daughter!"

All at once, the shrill of a loud chilling outcry disrupts their moment together and fills the ears of everyone else around as well.

The ten warriors become anxious and rush into the courthouse and when the others try to go in with them, King Liam decrees, "Let them be as we must not disrupt the boundaries of what is now their own affairs."

Pine emerges from the courthouse a few moments later and looks on King Liam. He begs his forgiveness with tears in is eyes, "My confidence has been as sand. I've had no peace as stability was never found 'til trusting in your Great One and he has given me both of them. I am sorry for all the pain that I have caused. For you have been a light of truth which has allowed me to see that I have been feeding off a heart of stone while believing it was life. It is now known to me that spirits living in darkness attempted to disrupt the kingdom of heavenly peace. I thank you for your life which now gives me life. You are a testimony indeed.

"A notable change has taken place within your countenance and those who shine with you, Pine."

The other warriors who have gathered around see what has happened and brought out of darkness it allows them to comprehend Truth's light. The people of Eridu receive sight from their changes of hearts which open to join them in mind.

Prince Ronan appears with Cunna right behind him, "Grandfather!" He runs over and gives him a long hug while crying, "I thought that I would never see you again."

The warrior townsmen become aware of what has happened when the joy from Pine and the other ten men spills over, causing them to become more fervently involved. Gray then speaks for everyone, "Love has been chosen to fill us with life to replace our strife. For once we were in a place of darkest death within a hatred that kept us from seeing the best of life. King Liam has allowed us to sees that his choices of mercy, even after what we did, has built a home for us that is safe to trust in. The truth of the Great One, which is not deniable, has become identifiable inside our emotions to where light is no longer apart from our sight. We were supplied a land that we can call our own and this is not taken lightly."

Cunna speaks out, "I agree and as our leader, I move that Prince Ronan of Calington be crowned King; that he may flourish to exceed King Liam's wisdom among us as a payment that will reward all provinces throughout the lands. We shall all glean from the light of his relationship with life as his bond has met with God's seed of intimacy joined in love. For I have discovered that his blood is akin to us both in natural and of spiritual descent."

"As the voice of our people, I second that he be our king!" says Gray.

"…And I as Magistrate shall draft this into our bylaws to be signed by us all."

King Liam looks over at his grandson, "Remember Ronan, now that you too shall be a prince of a king over your own province, let your love for God guide you. For when the truth of clear blue eyes turn to gold, a heart can easily become cool and turn black."

"Can mother stay with me, grandfather?"

"Ha! Of course."

Cunna then states, "We shall have a palace built for you."

Couldn't I just stay at your house? For I would rather not be separated from the people and lose touch with those whom I shall serve.

For as you have suggested, grandfather, if my heart doth not remain pliable with love in the presence of others, then something will go terribly wrong."

King Liam ponders to himself for a minute and looking over to his grandson, he signals to the keeper of the royal records by pointing at him, "Hand them over."

"What are these records for?"

"I noticed your apprehension at first when coming over to me before the courthouse. These records are so you will understand why I could not come to see you after you were found."

"I did become confused about the way love can separate itself for a season and still be remembered as being there. Yes, I was lost in a darkness 'til remembering that regardless of what can happen in life, true love remains to be carried from within …"

"…Or, can be reunited when we are glorified in heaven without a return to it on earth again, Ronan."

Learning to be patient and wait on the timing of God has allowed me to see with an understanding of why you could not be there at all times."

With this revelation, Ronan loves The Great One even more and lets out a shout, "Hallelujah!"

His grandfather then tells him, "I will visit with you and your mother once a week to maintain our friendship. For I am sure that you will have much to teach me, too, while learning what it is to be a king.

Pine looks over to Princess Suzy, "I can find no words to describe what I have put you and your family through. I only know that there must be much that hurts in the dark that needs to be brought to light that you may heal. Whatever you deem best, I will do."

"There is much to consider, I will pray."

King Henry clears his throat before speaking, "Now, what is it that you are going to teach me by your first command, Ronan?"

"If I am a king? I suppose I should wear a crown, but who will make it?"

"We do have a blacksmith here in town," says Pine.

"I shall go and find him."

Cunna suggests, "Ah, majesty. That's not exactly how it works."

Pine then states, "Because you are king, you're to bid for people to come to you."

"I thought that the greatest among us was the servant to all."

King Liam intervenes, "If you have to keep going every place, what would happen if while you were away an important decision needed to be made right away?"

"I guess I shall need lots of messengers then."

"Why?"

"I cannot be every place to meet my peoples needs and must know what is going on, grandfather."

"You should know that those who you trust to listen to for advice are called Advisor's and the advisers who travel for you with wisdom to negotiate terms to get what is needed for the good of the people are called ambassadors. There are others who deliver local messages for the court as well, these are called couriers.

"Where are they?"

"You have to choose them. Know that when you have a problem, pray and ask God for wisdom. When he answers, your solution will come."

"Oh, I see I have a lot of praying to do."

"Cunna volunteers, "You can use my messengers on a trial basis 'til you can choose some of your own, if you're not happy with them then they can be replaced."

"Thank you, oh Great One, for knowing my heart."

Cunna nods his head in approval.

"I guess that makes you an advisor, Cunna."

"If that's what you want, majesty?"

"A party. I say we shall have a party like at my birthday. It shall be in celebration of me receiving my crown. Young maidens shall be invited from every province for all the men to make friends, 'For it is not good for man to be alone.'"

"That should put the men on your good side," says Pine.

Ronan speaks in a low tone of voice which prevents the other warriors from hearing, "No, this shall be a test to see how the men behave with the women. If they respect them by honoring God with proposals for marriage, it will show that they'll be trust worthy and loyal to me. If they get out of line,

I know a jail that will hold them 'til they calm down if need be."

The Magistrate shows more remorse for his earlier behavior, "Ronan, an apology is in order for my actions. Thank God for the mercy of his angels or I'd still be under the power of that Dark Sorceress …"

" …Father, I forgive you for what you tried to do to me. I further understand that those who do not have a true relationship with The Great One can only strive for what this world has to offer as eyes turn to gold instead of the truth of love."

Pine kisses his son's hand and says, "I thank you."

Ronan interrupts the moment, "Now what was that about a dark sorceress?"

"In our old country, the darkness came to me in the form of a mighty warrior that gave me a sense of power every time I completed a conquest. It seemed to cause me to grow more powerful with every violent act, but it was all lies. As in the end, I was able to see the deception within the light of the greater power of love."

Cunna becomes involved, "I was there, too. For we both experienced a hatred that drew us into a distain that tried to suck our lives down into an open and dark abyss."

"I see that by Cunna agreeing to carry my burden with you in prayer, I have escaped this darkness. The Great One's powerful mercy of blood has defeated what was void at the inception of dawn of everything conceivable.

"Tell me how it has changed form on discovering this evil in our country?" asks King Liam.

"It awakened me to a seduction which caused me to feel as though I could judge in place of God's love. It lied by telling me that the truth of our old ways was greater than mercy. For I was convinced that there was no beauty in showing mercy and if it existed I was weak."

"Meek is not weak as wisdom is greater than all judgments that doth not trust in God's plan. So, we must not try to implement one through a pride of our own with a mind less compassion of heart as this will always open the door to a fruit of evil. You shall learn from our *Book of Life* that it took just one bite of this rotten fruit, which was incomplete at its core to cut off the bloodline of light and life. It has steered all men into what dies in the dark where once bit, the black door was open to replace the brilliance of light, allowing evil to become knowledgeable by choice."

Pine's eyes light in response, "Now I understand how the inception of this idea has led me to stray as I never knew that loving all of creation was there as the deeper way 'til the light of truth brought me back. I know where this evil outside my thoughts exists as it lurks in darkness within a room in the court house in a black robe even now. I cannot believe that it had my thoughts in such a confused state of mind that I enjoyed its darkness while communing with it."

Ronan asks, "You know where the leader of evil exists!"

King Liam speaks with wisdom, "We can only shut out the darkness of this evil by purity of light. One where we must enter with a walk against the pressure of its waves of perpetual motion. So, press in through the doorway of The Great One and our

Christ. He is our friend, our light, and all life by His own blood sacrifice.

"What is The Great One's name so that all may know him as a friend, too?" says Pine.

"Jesus, The Christ!"

"Wait! I know that name. You used it to grant me freedom by His light from all the darkness that had me chained as not to recognize myself with sight. What a poor creature I was when all the while I thought I was bright. For in being changed by God while walking in the freedom of brilliance when things get dark from clouds that storm, I am one who trusts by faith that He shall make all right. Now, how shall we contain this or any evil which always tries to manipulate by frights?"

Ronan remembers, "The priests told me about having blood on the door posts of a house for a death angel to pass by using the sacrificed blood of a lamb which was stated in the *Book of Life*. Perhaps if we were to use our sacrifice from the marriage supper of the lamb's table, His blood would keep it locked away by adoration. If we placed it before this door, could it keep the dark angel sealed inside? Would it not prevent any darkness from spreading to more minds?"

His grandfather answers him, "Darkness cannot be contained as evil rules by way of messengers while confined or not. We are all engulfed in this fallen world in which we live and except by each individual choice to receive Christ's light, darkness could not be destroyed. It will always take His living blood on our door posts while in time. For whoever seeks to remain in the purity of His light shall be guided by The Holy Spirit. So, let His blood flow on earth as it is in heaven giving any with faith eternal life. For words spoken in darkness can never truly be our friends as they all lead to not understand but only make pretend. A lie and the truth can never coexist as the truth of life states itself, 'What fellowship doth darkness have with light.'"

Pine then inquires, "We are to do nothing?"

King Liam patiently answers, "We are to stay focused on the light and mindful of our own business while being guided by our friend as having an axe to grind to prove a point takes away the joy of Holy light. The rest will always fall into place and work its way out as there be no more accusers to confuse, lest His gaze be removed from directing us. For only in this moment can The Great One speak for himself within the silence of the night."

About the Author

R. A. Feller is an internationally acclaimed award winning poet. A Veteran Writer who has written 18 books over a 40 year period. The first of the 9 book Calington Castle series has been hailed a classic and all are deemed outstanding. You are in for the adventure of your life.

Calingtoncastle.com